✳ The unicorn reared up and galloped away down one of the branching tunnels. Every single bullet missed its mark. No one made a move to follow the creature.

"Confound you, you popinjay!" Slaggingham bellowed. "You fairy-tale jumping jack! Drat you and that meddling Timothy Hunter!"

Daniel's face grew hot, and his heart thudded double time in his chest. "Did you say . . . did you say Timothy Hunter?" he gasped.

With several clicks, Slaggingham's weapon folded back into his coat. Slaggingham looked down at Daniel. "I did. Do you know him?"

"I'll say I do. He stole my girl, Marya." Daniel took a deep breath. "If you're against Timothy Hunter, then I'm your man. I hate him."

"So does that mean we have an agreement?" Slaggingham asked eagerly.

Daniel nodded, then thrust out his hand for the man to shake. "We does indeed." ✳

# the BOOKS of MAGIC *4

# Consequences

**Carla Jablonski**

Created by
**Neil Gaiman and John Bolton**

BOOKS FOR
**VERTIGO**
YOUNG ADULTS

eos

*An Imprint of* HarperCollins*Publishers*

Eos is an imprint of HarperCollins Publishers.

The Books of Magic: Summonings comic books were created by the following
people:

Written by John Ney Reiber
Illustrated by Gary Amaro, Dick Giordano, Peter Gross, and Peter Snejbjerg

This is a work of fiction. Any resemblance to any real people (living, dead, or
stolen by fairies), or to any real animals, gods, witches, countries, and events
(magical or otherwise), is just blind luck, or so we hope.

Library of Congress Cataloging-in-Publication Data
Jablonski, Carla.
    Consequences / Carla Jablonski.— 1st Eos ed.
        p.   cm. — (The books of magic ; #4)
    "Timothy Hunter and the Books of Magic created by Neil Gaiman and John
Bolton. Primarily adapted from the story serialized in the Books of Magic:
Summonings, originally published by Vertigo, 1994 and 1995."
    Summary: Thirteen-year-old Tim Hunter encounters danger in his own world, as
an angry visitor from another realm arrives in London seeking vengeance on the
young magician just as he is learning new things about his powers.
    ISBN 0-06-447382-1 (pbk.)
    [1. Magic—Fiction. 2. Wizards—Fiction. 3. London (England)—Fiction.]
I. Gaiman, Neil. II. Bolton, John, 1951– III. Books of magic. IV. Title.
PZ7.J1285 Con 2004                                           2003007679
[Fic]—dc21                                                        CIP
                                                                   AC

Typography by R. Hult
◆

First Eos edition, 2004
Visit us on the World Wide Web!
www.harpereos.com
www.dccomics.com

For Matthew and Michelle, just
because.
—CJ

# THE BOOKS OF MAGIC
## An Introduction

### by Neil Gaiman

WHEN I WAS STILL a teenager, only a few years older than Tim Hunter is in the book you are holding, I decided it was time to write my first novel. It was to be called *Wild Magic*, and it was to be set in a minor British Public School (which is to say, a private school), like the ones from which I had so recently escaped, only a minor British Public School that taught magic. It had a young hero named Richard Grenville, and a pair of wonderful villains who called themselves Mister Croup and Mister Vandemar. It was going to be a mixture of Ursula K. Le Guin's *A Wizard of Earthsea* and T. H. White's *The Sword in the Stone*, and, well, me, I suppose. That was the plan. It seemed to me that learning about magic was the perfect story, and I was sure I could really write convincingly about school.

I wrote about five pages of the book before I realized that I had absolutely no idea what I was doing, and I stopped. (Later, I learned that most books are actually written by people who have no idea what they are doing, but go on to finish writing the books anyway. I wish I'd known that then.)

Years passed. I got married, and had children of my own, and learned how to finish writing the things I'd started.

Then one day in 1988, the telephone rang.

It was an editor in America named Karen Berger. I had recently started writing a monthly comic called *The Sandman*, which Karen was editing, although no issues had yet been published. Karen had noticed that I combined a sort of trainspotterish knowledge of minor and arcane DC Comics characters with a bizarre facility for organizing them into something more or less coherent. And also, she had an idea.

"Would you write a comic," she asked, "that would be a history of magic in the DC Comics universe, covering the past and the present and the future? Sort of a Who's Who, but with a story? We could call it *The Books of Magic*."

I said, "No, thank you." I pointed out to her how silly an idea it was—a Who's Who and a history and a travel guide that was also a story. "Quite a ridiculous idea," I said, and she apologized for having suggested it.

In bed that night I hovered at the edge of sleep, musing about Karen's call, and what a ridiculous idea it was. I mean . . . a story that would go from the beginning of time . . . to the end of time . . . and have someone meet all these strange people . . . and learn all about magic. . . .

Perhaps it wasn't so ridiculous. . . .

And then I sighed, certain that if I let myself sleep it would all be gone in the morning. I climbed out of bed and crept through the house back to my office, trying not to wake anyone in my hurry to start scribbling down ideas.

A boy. Yes. There had to be a boy. Someone smart and funny, something of an outsider, who would learn that he had the potential to be the greatest magician the world had ever seen—more powerful than Merlin. And four guides, to take him through the past, the present, through other worlds, through the future, serving the same function as the ghosts who accompany Ebenezer Scrooge through Charles Dickens's *A Christmas Carol.*

I thought for a moment about calling him Richard Grenville, after the hero of my book-I'd-never-written, but that seemed a rather too heroic name (the original Sir Richard Grenville was a sea captain, adventurer, and explorer, after all). So I called him Tim, possibly because the Monty

Python team had shown that Tim was an unlikely sort of name for an enchanter, or with faint memories of the hero of Margaret Storey's magical children's novel, *Timothy and Two Witches*. I thought perhaps his last name should be Seekings, and it was, in the first outline I sent to Karen—a faint tribute to John Masefield's haunting tale of magic and smugglers, *The Midnight Folk*. But Karen felt this was a bit literal, so he became, in one stroke of the pen, Tim Hunter.

And as Tim Hunter he sat up, blinked, wiped his glasses on his T-shirt, and set off into the world.

(I never actually got to use the minor British Public School that taught only magic in a story, and I suppose now I never will. But I was very pleased when Mr. Croup and Mr. Vandemar finally showed up in a story about life under London, called *Neverwhere*.)

John Bolton, the first artist to draw Tim, had a son named James who was just the right age and he became John's model for Tim, tousle-haired and bespectacled. And in 1990 the first four volumes of comics that became the first *Books of Magic* graphic novel were published.

Soon enough, it seemed, Tim had a monthly series of comics chronicling his adventures and misadventures, and the slow learning process he was to undergo, as initially chronicled by author John Ney Reiber, who gave Tim a number of things—most importantly, Molly.

In this new series of novels-without-pictures, Carla Jablonski has set herself a challenging task: not only adapting Tim's stories, but also telling new ones, and through it all illuminating the saga of a young man who might just grow up to be the most powerful magician in the world. If, of course, he manages to live that long. . . .

*Neil Gaiman*
*May 2002*

# Prologue

## Free Country

IT WAS ANOTHER GLORIOUS DAY in Free Country, a spectacular afternoon in an eternity of blissful hours. All was well in the sanctuary world, originally created as a haven for children in danger. The lovely spirits who were the heart and soul of this paradise, the Shimmers, danced above their crystalline pond. Children's laughter could be heard punctuating the soundscape, mingled with lapping water, rushing brooks, birdcalls, and wind chimes. This was a world where the formerly deprived, the previously abused, and the perpetually frightened could be happy and safe. Yes, all was as it should be, as it always was.

Or was it?

Daniel sat glumly in a rickety little rowboat, glaring at his fishing pole. His long dark blond hair was pulled back in a ponytail that poked out from under the battered top hat sitting low on his forehead. He had rolled up his striped cotton trousers and his overcoat sleeves so they wouldn't get wet, but they did anyway. This did not improve his mood.

"Any luck?" Spud asked.

Spud perched in the bow of the boat, facing Daniel, with his fishing line over the side. Daniel was in the stern, gazing unseeing at the high cliffs rising from the riverbanks. It had been Spud's stupid idea to go fishing. Daniel wasn't going to let him get off lightly for such a bad plan.

"Not a nibble," Daniel complained. "You know, Spud, it would help if we had some bait on them hooks."

"Cripes, Daniel," Spud replied. "Any ol' gump can catch fishies with bait! And here I thought you was a sport."

"I'll tell you what I am," Daniel grumbled. "I'm stunning bored, that's what."

"Awww, ain't you a drip and a half," Spud complained. "You're a regular wet blanket these days. Ever since your sweetie pie scrammed out of here."

"Marya wasn't my—" Daniel whirled around on the bench, nearly capsizing the little boat. He settled himself before he continued. "We was *friends*. That's all."

Spud snorted. "Sure. You were just pals. 'Cause she wouldn't have anything to do with the likes of you."

Daniel turned back around in his seat, so that Spud couldn't see his face. He fixed his eyes on a spot on the horizon and counted to ten. His hands balled into fists, despite his effort to stay calm. "What do you know?" he muttered.

"I know more than you think," Spud taunted. "The way I heard it, Marya ran away because you tried to kiss her."

"What?" Daniel rose from the bench without even thinking. He turned and stepped in front of Spud, scowling down at the boy.

"Quit rocking the boat, will you? Do you want to end up in the water?" Spud scolded.

"You take that back," Daniel ordered. He knew he shouldn't let Spud get to him like this— that it would only egg Spud on. But the things he was saying! Daniel couldn't just let that pass.

As predicted, Spud smirked and kept up with his teasing. "Yep. I heard you snuck up on her at Shimmer Rock and gave her a great big ol' smackaroonie! She burst into tears and ran away, clear out of Free Country."

Daniel reached down and grabbed Spud's upper arm.

"Ow!" Spud yelped. "Let go!"

Daniel yanked Spud up off his seat so that they were nose to nose. "You listen to me," Daniel growled. His voice was low and serious. He didn't think he had ever heard himself sound that way before. "I never did no such thing."

For the first time, he saw real fear in Spud's brown eyes. The boy squirmed, trying to get away, and knocked his tweed cap into the water. "Let go," Spud said—only this time it wasn't a command, it was a plea.

Daniel just clenched tighter, with both hands now. Spud stopped struggling and went limp in Daniel's grip.

"You think Marya's gone because of something I done?" Daniel demanded, giving Spud a little shake. "What do you think she took with her as her most special memento? Huh?" He shook Spud again. "The little ballerina statue I gave her. What do you think of that!"

He released Spud, who teetered and then sat down hard on the bench, water sloshing up into the rowboat. Daniel bent his knees a bit, rocking with the boat, keeping his balance.

Spud rubbed his arm and scowled at Daniel. "Okay, okay, you don't have to get all physical."

Daniel knew Spud would have a big bruise on his arm, but he didn't care. Spud had to learn that he couldn't say such things and get away with it.

"So then why *did* Marya leave?" Spud asked moodily.

Daniel's eyes narrowed. He felt anger rise up in him again, only this time it wasn't Spud he was mad at. "It was that Timothy Hunter," he said with a clenched jaw. "Timothy Hunter lured her away to the Bad World and I hate him for it."

"So why don't you go and get her back, instead of picking on me," Spud complained, rubbing his arm again.

Daniel stared at Spud. He had never realized what a genius Spud was until that minute. He was dead brilliant!

Sitting down beside Spud on the little bench, Daniel clapped a hand on Spud's shoulder. Spud flinched, as if he were afraid Daniel would hurt him again.

"That's just what I intend to do, old chap," Daniel said to Spud, giving him a friendly squeeze. "I'll find her, all right. I'll find that bloody Tim, too. Timothy Hunter will regret the day he ever came to Free Country."

# Chapter One

"SO YOU SEE, MOLLY, it's like this." Timothy Hunter took a deep breath and launched into his speech. "I am the greatest, most powerful magician of all time. At least"—he ducked his head modestly—"that's what they tell me."

Tim paused and then groaned. *You sound like a head-swollen, egomaniacal loon*, he scolded himself.

Timothy Hunter, the boy with the potential to wield extraordinary magic, skate-boarded back and forth in front of Molly O'Reilly's dilapidated house. He'd been doing it for about half an hour. He and Molly had planned to meet later, and he was determined to have this conversation today. He tried out different speeches as he carefully avoided the many cracks that spread like veins in the pavement. In this part of London, a bloke was lucky if the traffic lights worked and the garbage was picked up regularly. Asking for smooth asphalt was a bit much. Tim didn't mind—he developed his awesome boarding skills by learning not to let such obstacles trip him up.

He arrived at the end of the street and rolled to a stop. "Try again," he told himself, picking up the board and turning it around. "Version number three hundred and twelve." He kicked himself along until he picked up speed, then balanced expertly as he dodged cracks, litter, and a mangy stray dog.

"Okay, Molly, you're probably not going to believe me, but I swear on anything you like it's true," he declared. "I didn't believe it at first either. But these guys—I call them the Trenchcoat Brigade—came and gave me the heads up on being magic."

He flipped up onto the sidewalk as a car drove past him, spraying some gray slush—the last bit of slush from the winter. "I've been to other worlds," he continued. "I even saved a few."

He frowned. Every time he tried telling even imaginary Molly about some of the truly stupendous things he'd done, he had to stop. It sounded impossible and worse—it sounded like bragging. Then he wound up feeling like a total fake, because he wasn't always certain *how* he had done the things he had done.

Take Free Country for instance, he thought.

The kids there had kind of kidnapped him, wanting to use his power to save the place. But instead, he'd short-circuited everything. Literally—major power eruptions. The weirdest thing was, that *was* what ultimately saved them. Tim had protected that world by accident. He was glad he had—he just didn't know how he'd done it.

What if Molly asked him to prove that he was magic? She was definitely an I'll-believe-it-when-I-see-it kind of girl. Her down-to-earth, no-nonsense attitude was one of the qualities he liked best about her. That and the fact that she was super tough, really brave, and awfully funny. He liked her soft-looking hair and sparkling brown eyes. Even more important, she was someone he could talk to. Like when he found out that the man who raised him wasn't really his father. She'd come through aces when he'd told her. High marks in all categories.

Only, even then, he had held something back. Something big. He didn't let her in on the fact that he had also found out who his real father was: a man named Tamlin, who lived in a completely different world called Faerie and could turn himself into a bird. Tim had left out that little feathered detail when he talked to Molly.

"I should have told her everything right then," he muttered. Was she going to be angry that he'd waited so long to tell her? He'd never kept a secret like this from her before. It had been almost six months since the Trenchcoat Brigade episode, and she still didn't know. The snow was melting, the ground turned to soggy mud, and tiny little buds were starting their willful attempt to grow in this concrete and asphalt world, and still Tim had not told her.

So much had happened so fast—time seemed to move differently for him now. It had moved differently that first day—or was it a first lifetime?—when the Trenchcoat Brigade had appeared out of nowhere to lay this whammy on him. They'd taken him to the past, the present, and even into the future, only to deposit him back in the here and now—only the here and now had been forever changed for him. "Here" now included unseen gates, passageways into other worlds, worlds that bordered on his own, and "now" meant one thing in this world and quite something else in any other. That made it hard to tell how much time had passed during any of his adventures. When Tim had saved Faerie from the grip of the evil manticore, Molly hadn't missed him at all. As far as she could tell, he'd been gone only a few short hours, yet Tim had been to death and back again. It had felt like days, weeks, even months.

It was all so impossible, and yet it had all happened. No wonder he'd been having trouble finding the words to tell Molly. It was a delicate situation to explain. Tim tried it out loud. "I know you think you know me, but you don't, because I hardly know myself." He shook his head. That wasn't something a girl would like to hear. *Yes*, he thought, *the words have to be just right.*

*You make the choice to believe in magic,* Tim mused. *To be magic. To live in a magic world. But nothing turns out the way you expect. And you've got no one to turn to, no one to show you. No teacher. No parent. No one but yourself to count on—unless you tell Molly.*

Tim pulled up short. Was he being selfish in wanting to tell her? Was his real reason so that there would be somebody he could share this burdensome gift with? He knew Molly couldn't show him the ropes; he'd need someone magic to do that. Someone like the magician Zatanna or John Constantine of the Trenchcoat Brigade. But neither of them had offered to be his magic tutor. He had this weird feeling, though, that he and Molly could figure it out together. But was that fair? He seemed to be continually risking death whenever he encountered a magic world, creature, or adventure. Did he have the right to drag her into danger, too?

Tim snorted. He could just hear Molly. "That's for me to decide, isn't it, Hunter? Just give me the facts and I'll make up my own mind." She'd be a lot angrier if she found out he'd been keeping something this big from her, never mind the danger involved.

"Okay, so today's the day," Tim muttered. "You've been working up the courage since this whole thing started. Now do it!"

He rolled past her door one more time. He wanted to be sure he could explain it so that she wouldn't question his sanity. He wanted her to know from the very beginning that what he was saying was true. But how could he do that?

"Evidence!" Tim declared, rolling to a stop. "I should figure out some kind of magic to do to prove to Molly that it's all true. That way she'll know I haven't gone 'round the bend." *Just one problem*, he reminded himself. *You don't really have a clue about what you're doing. If I could just get in some practice time*, he thought. *But where I can I do that kind of homework?*

Then it came to him. The abandoned lot. It had been his favorite place to think when he was a little kid. No one ever went there. He'd be alone, and he was pretty sure there wouldn't be anything there that he could blow up or break. It was the perfect place to work on magic. He needed to

know how to direct this overwhelming power so
that he controlled *it* rather than the other way
around. And then he could come up with something really snazzy to show Molly.

He checked his watch. *I still have some time
before meeting Molly*, he decided, then skated the
few blocks over to the vacant lot. It was overgrown with weeds, but the big spreading oak tree
still loomed as large as a castle. Pieces of junk—
rusting car parts, a bicycle wheel, a shoe—peeked
up out of the tall grass and litter.

It looked a lot worse than he'd remembered.
*Everything changes*, he noted, *especially childhood
hideaways*.

"All right, Tim," he muttered to himself. "So
it was dumb coming here." He sat down on his
board and rested his elbows on his knees. When
he was a kid, he had really believed this was the
best and safest place to be. He had even had a
group of little imaginary friends he'd hang out
with here.

"It really bites," he grumbled. "You stop
believing in safe places about the time you start to
need them."

"Hey there, Hunter," a boy called. "I'd stay
clear of that lot if I were you, chap."

Tim turned around and saw Scott Whitman, a
fellow skater, kick his board up neatly to catch it.

He was about a year older than Tim and went to a different school, but boarding made them friendly. He had a blond buzz cut, and wore his baggy trousers low. Tucking his skateboard under his arm, he shoved his hands into the pockets of his windbreaker.

"Hey." Tim stood and greeted Scott. "What's wrong with the lot?"

"I had Darlene out here the other night, hoping for some privacy," Scott explained. "Between her parents, the guard dogs, and my stupid brothers we never get any chance alone, you know?"

Tim didn't, but he nodded anyway.

Scott took a few steps into the tall grass of the lot. He laid his board on the pavement and held it still with one foot as he surveyed the area. He seemed to be troubled by the place.

"So what happened?" Tim asked.

"We're in there, Darlene and me, and we're heading for the big tree, but we stop. I'm hearing stuff in the grass. Rustling. Like someone or something's following us. Then Darlene says it ain't just grass she's hearing."

"What was it?" Tim's eyebrows rose.

"She thinks it's something whispering. Only we can't see it." Scott knelt down and rummaged in the grass. "Where'd the bloody thing go?" he muttered. "I know I chucked it right about here. Oh, here it is." He held something out to Tim. "Then she steps on this, and we hear a nasty laugh."

Scott stood and plopped the object into Tim's hand. "We got out of there right quick, I tell you."

Tim stared down at the object in horror.

# Chapter Two

*IT COULDN'T BE*, TIM told himself. He was holding a little head in his hands. It looked as if it might have once belonged to some kind of elf or sprite. As far as he could make out, its face, its ears, and its hair all would have blended easily into the woods, as if it were designed to be camouflaged. But the little head had been cruelly severed from its body, and its mouth still seemed to be howling in pain. It had also been burned, and flecks of soot and ash came off in Tim's hand.

"Whoa," Tim murmured.

"Yeah," Scott agreed. "Sick, isn't it? Somebody making a cute little thing like that just to chop it up and burn it. Like it was garbage or something."

Scott picked up his skateboard. "Like I said, I'm not sticking around this place. I don't want to meet the dude who thought that was fun. You coming?"

Tim never took his eyes off the little head. "No, thanks," he replied. "I've got stuff to do."

Scott shrugged. "Suit yourself."

"Thanks for the warning," Tim called after Scott. The older boy quickly skate-boarded around the corner and vanished.

Tim stared at the head. It was more than eerie—it was familiar. He recognized the face. "Is it really you?" he asked it. For in his hand he held none other than Tibby, one of his imaginary playmates from when Tim was a little kid. Or what was left of him.

*Why would anyone kill an imaginary playmate?* Tim wondered. *Hold on—how do imaginary playmates become real in the first place?* He had never tried to make a doll of Tibby, as he had with some of his other fanciful ideas. So how could he be holding this physical manifestation in his hands?

He scanned the lot and realized that it had changed somehow while he'd been standing there. The tree had grown larger, the grass taller. The area had expanded, so that he couldn't see to the end of it. Yet just a minute ago the brick back wall of the Furniture King had been quite visible.

"Uh-oh," Tim murmured. "Here we go again." There was magic here. Was it the place? Was it him? Was it someone else here? He'd have to find out.

He took a few steps deeper into the lot and realized it now looked the way it had back when he was about five years old, when he had spent the most time here. The grass once again came up to his chest the way it used to.

He made his way deeper into the lot, pushing the tall weeds aside, trying not to trip over odd bits of trash.

"Really, Tim, if you must go wandering into fairy tales, why not try for something a bit nicer?" he scolded himself. He stepped over a pile of soggy and shredding newspapers. "Or at least something where you know the outcome in advance and are guaranteed a happy ending. Something with talking bears and porridge, say." He sighed. "Almost anything would beat slogging through a place you made up when you were four, trying to find out what killed your imaginary pal."

He arrived at the base of the enormous tree, and stared at its complex root system, its peeling bark. He squinted at the little head again.

"Let's see," he addressed the head. "You were the Narl who threw acorns at people I didn't like." Tim remembered the times he sat hiding in the tree, wishing he were brave enough to hurl acorns at the kids who picked on him. Sometimes, an acorn actually fell on its own and beaned one of the bullies, and Tim always attributed it to the Narl named Tibby. He'd imagine Tibby beside him on the tree branch, blending in with the bark. He'd picture Tibby shimmying to the very end of the branch and tossing down the acorns.

Tim shook his head, feeling a slight blush rise in his cheeks as he remembered all his childhood pretendings. "How embarrassing. What's the point of growing up if you can't leave behind all that kid stuff?"

He gently laid the little head to rest at the base of the tree. "There used to be a lot of my imaginary Narls down here," he remembered. "One used to hide my glasses for me when I didn't want to wear them. One used to turn me invisible when I knew Mum was serving deviled Spam for lunch." He got on his hands and knees and peered into the hole in the base of the tree. "And one— Hey!"

Suddenly Tim was knocked over by tiny hands. He sat back up and saw two little creatures glaring at him. They looked like they were made from bits of tree and grass—little pointy twigs stuck out of their heads, their limbs were spiky and splintery, and their skin . . . could it be *bark*? They were only about six inches high, but they looked as if they could prick a person like a porcupine. These were more of the Narls he had imagined, like Tibby.

Wondering what the little creatures would do, Tim sat up slowly and cautiously. After all, a bloke never knew what magical creatures were capable of, no matter how small and cute they looked.

"Stand clear, Tanger," one of them ordered. He held a branch over one shoulder like a baseball bat. "Ooh, I'll give him such a whack!"

"Er, pardon me, Crimple?" the one called Tanger said. He pushed his little spectacles farther up the bridge of his long pointy nose. He was a few inches shorter than plump Crimple. Both had moss and grass covering their bodies like fur. "Hang on a second."

Crimple ignored him. He took a few tiny steps toward Tim. "I'll teach him to go peering and prying in decent folk's trees. The worm."

"Crimple!" Tanger said more forcefully. This time Crimple looked at Tanger. The wee woody creature sidled up to Crimple and whispered hoarsely behind a splintery hand. "That's the Opener himself you're calling a worm. Or I'm a saucepan!" He stared down at the ground, rocking back and forth on his tiny feet.

"The Opener?" Crimple lowered his twig weapon. His little eyes went wide. "Oh, my brittle spittle spattle. Mercy me!"

He gaped at Tim, while Tanger smiled sheepishly. Tim took a long look at the woody creatures, hiding a smile. For such cute little critters, they were awfully feisty and fierce. He admired that.

"I know you," Tim exclaimed. He pointed at Tanger. "You used to hide my glasses."

Tanger placed a hand on his chest and bowed his head. "And a great honor it was, your benevolence, I'm sure."

"Oh, pish posh!" Crimple sputtered. "You haven't been here long enough to polish a perishing root, Tanger, much less pinch spectacles. None of us have!"

Their disagreement on the basic facts of their existence surprised Tim. "How long have you been here?" he asked.

"Ages and ages, your worship, or I'm a colander!" replied Tanger.

"Piffle!" Crimple exclaimed. "Five moons and not a sliver more!"

Five moons? Tim realized that meant five months. That was about the time he'd had his visit from the Trenchcoat Brigade.

"Five moons?" Tanger repeated. "Five moons? That is highly unlikely, given the pleasant memories I have of the Opener."

"Memories?" Crimple scoffed. "What have you to remember, you who are barely here?"

"I am as here as you are!" Tanger objected. "Or I'm a cheese grater!"

Crimple held up his hands in a placating gesture. "All right, old friend, perhaps I'm slightly off
the mark. I haven't really been myself of late."

Tim listened to them argue, trying to figure
out what was going on. If Tanger truly was the
Narl he remembered, he'd have been here for
years. But Crimple didn't agree with that time
frame. Then again, time did funny things when
magic was involved. And why did they call him the
Opener?

Tanger held up a pointy wooden finger. "If I
may offer a solution to solve this perplexing
riddle," Tanger said. "Perhaps we *were* here, and
then we returned."

"If that's the case, splinter head," Crimple
said, "where did we go?"

Tanger's mouth opened, then shut. They both
turned to Tim and waited for him to come up with
an answer.

Tim shrugged. "I think Tanger's on the right
track," he said. Tanger gave Crimple a smug
smile. "I think you were my friends when I was
small and then you went into kind of a hibernation
and recently woke back up." *Just around the same
time my magic was woken up by the Trenchcoat
Brigade. Go figure.*

"All right, you two," Tim said, clambering
back up to his feet. "I came in here because I

found one of you out there, and he had been—
well, destroyed. I want to know what happened to
him. And something else." He put his hands on his
hips and scanned the overgrown lot. "This place
isn't quite the way I remember it. This junk was
never here, for one thing." He kicked an old tire.

"No, Master Opener. I suppose it wasn't," said
Tanger. "I expect the Wobbly was a bit more dis-
creet about feathering its nest back then."

"Hey, how'd you know about the Wobbly?"
Tim asked. "It was a funny little bird-headed
thing, right? And I used to feed it, uhmm . . ." he
trailed off, trying to remember.

"You fed it bread crusts," Crimple finished for
him. "And pieces of toys that bored you. Broken
shoestrings and old clothes."

"Things you didn't have any use for," Tanger
added. "Things you'd outgrown. Like you've outgrown us."

A dark shadow overhead made Tim shiver.
His nose wrinkled as a foul odor filled the air and
a rustling sound came closer and closer. Tim
glanced up at the sky, and his mouth dropped
open.

A vulturelike creature was approaching, huge
flapping wings creating a stench-filled breeze.
Instead of bone, flesh, and feathers, this bird of
prey was made of garbage—odds and ends and

junk. It let out an ugly *caw*! and with every flap of
its grotesque wings, pieces dropped off, as if it
were falling apart. Held together by muck and
dust, dirt and debris, it swooped down, reached
out its talons, and grabbed Tanger.

In horror, Tim realized that this . . . this . . .
*thing* was the Wobbly, a creature he himself had
invented to get rid of stuff.

The Wobbly hovered above the ground,
Tanger dangling in its powerful grip. "What's the
use of growing up," it rasped in a terrible imper-
sonation of Tim, "if you can't leave behind all this
kid stuff."

"Tanger! No!" Crimple jumped up and down,
trying to grab Tanger's tiny foot, but he couldn't
reach it.

The Wobbly threw back its head and let out
another skin-tingling *caw*. It flapped its wings and
started to move away.

"Stop!" Tim shouted.

The garbage vulture paused and perched on a
tree limb. "You cry stop, Opener? To me? You
opened the way between realms; you opened the
door between thought and action, imagination and
reality. You made me to serve your purpose. And
you tell me now to stop?"

"Wobbly, listen. What you said just now—"

"Is what you said a moment ago."

"I may have thought that, but I didn't mean it. Not the way you do. Put Tanger down."

"These useless ones." The Wobbly lifted its talon and waved Tanger in front of Tim. "These useless ones and I, we came back again with the new magic that comes from you."

"Me?" Tim took a step backward. So it was true. They called him the Opener because that's what his magic did: It opened up possibilities. When he had chosen the path of magic, these creatures had popped back into existence, suddenly wholly real.

The Wobbly swung Tanger back and forth. The little wood man's eyes were round with terror behind his spectacles. He was too afraid even to scream.

"The useless ones shape themselves from your old way of thinking," the Wobbly snarled. "But I shape me from the new. I do not stop, Opener. I do not put down. I am keeper of the new way. I work for you as you are now." With its free talon, it pulled a ragged, rusty hacksaw from somewhere amid the garbage that was its body. "You are done with these. They are useless. To be discarded. Destroyed."

Crimple threw twigs at the Wobbly, then grass, and even clumps of dirt. But his hands were so tiny that all he could throw were little bits that the Wobbly never even noticed.

*Do something*, Tim admonished himself. *Say something. Six-inch Crimple is fighting back. So should you.*

"It is my mission to rid the world of the useless," the Wobbly continued. "For this you made me. You have outgrown them, so these will be destroyed. As I destroyed the one you called Tibby."

"You're doing this all wrong," Tim said, hoping he sounded sure of himself. "We don't burn our rubbish or saw it into little bits anymore."

That caught the Wobbly's attention. "No?"

*Keep it up*, Tim told himself. *You can handle the old vulture. You made it out of sticks and rags when you were five years old, remember? How bright can it be?*

"Sawing up throw-aways, burning them— that's considered very old-fashioned," Tim scoffed. "*Recycling* is the new thing."

The Wobbly pulled its head back and clicked its beak a few times. "What means this, Opener? Re-cy-cling?"

"It means finding new uses for the useless," Tim explained. "It means keeping the useless in one piece and letting it find a new purpose, a new way to be useful again. So nothing ever has to be chopped up or burned."

"Yes! Recycling is all the rage these days," Crimple said, nodding quickly several times.

"Beautiful concept, hey?" said Tanger. His voice shook, but he smiled as if he didn't have a care in the world. "Quite ingenious, really. Or I'm a teapot."

"*Hrawwwwww*," the Wobbly cawed as if it were thinking. "*Crawwwwww*."

"Now if you'll just put me down," Tanger said eagerly, "I'll pitch myself under the, ah, good old recycling tree. And I can get right to work finding a new use for myself."

The Wobbly dropped Tanger to the ground. "Go, useless. And I go. To wait for other rubbish that has no purpose."

The Wobbly lifted off the branch, shaking the leaves. It trailed tin cans and old shoes and bits of half-eaten hamburger as it flew away.

"Much obliged, your Wobbly-ship," Tanger called after the garbage vulture.

Crimple dashed over to Tanger and threw his stiff, splintery arms around him. Tanger patted Crimple's shoulder and grinned at Tim.

"And, young master," Tanger said, "if you ever need someone to hide those glasses for you, you can count on me."

Tim smiled. "Thanks. I'll definitely keep you in mind."

He watched the little fellows stroll back into their tree, and shook his head, unsure of what had happened. He just knew that it had been important somehow.

*So you make a choice to believe in magic*, he mused. *And suddenly everything you've ever believed in matters. Everything you've ever done has consequences. Hanging a rag on a stick and calling it a Wobbly, for instance.* "Sheesh," he muttered. It was a lot of pressure.

Tim searched through the tall grass and found the original Wobbly he'd made so long ago, now much the worse for wear. Its rag head was shredded, and its stick body was bent and warped. He squatted down and studied it.

*Should I take this out of the lot and bury it or something?* he wondered. *Would that unmake it? Or would it just change it— maybe release it in a new and more dangerous form?* The Wobbly had certainly grown into something monstrous, though he wasn't quite sure what kind of danger it posed.

Tim decided the safest thing to do was leave the original Wobbly where it was. *I'd better mind my thoughts more closely*, he realized. *Who knows what wishes might come true, otherwise?*

He began to slowly make his way out of the lot. There were a great deal of memories here.

*When I was little I had to create imaginary*

*friends and creatures to do the things I wanted to do.
I needed the Wobbly to get rid of things for me. I
needed Tanger and Crimple to let me be mad at someone or avoid what I didn't want to do. Now I have to
face things dead-on, don't I?*

Face things dead-on. "Oh no!" he cried. "I'm
late to meet Molly!"

# Chapter Three

*Faerie*

KING AUBERON OF FAERIE sat on a high-backed, richly upholstered chair. In front of him, sprites and Fair Folk danced on the lush green lawn, his splendid castle looming above them. His wife, Queen Titania, led them in a merry quadrille, her long hair bouncing as she frolicked. The lilting melodies plucked on lutes, the rhythms of the drums and sticks did not set his slippered feet to dancing. He watched lovely winged creatures flit in and out of the dappled shadows of twilight; teasing, laughing, offering any sort of pleasure. But he was not tempted. Not by the food, the drink, the women, the songs. Nothing.

He was unhappy. Titania had grown even more distant. He never would have imagined such indifference to be possible when they had first wed. But now everything that was between them was heavy with failed expectations and secrets. She had taken the death of her Falconer, Tamlin, hard, harder than a Queen should over a courtier. First she was wracked by sobs, then filled with rage, and now, the desperate, endless amusements. Auberon could no longer pretend; he recognized that her reaction was that of a lover losing her beloved.

Auberon felt an unusual pang. Could it be jealousy? He shook it off. Titania had had her diversions through the years; he certainly had had his. What was one more in a long line of favorites?

And yet her agony over Tamlin's death made him wonder. Had there been something more . . . *real* between Titania and Tamlin than there was between Titania and himself? Would Titania have reacted this way if something had happened to *him*?

He observed the pretty scene before him, irritation prickling just beneath his blue skin. She held this fete as a way to distract herself from her loss. But her laughter had become shrill and forced; Auberon remembered a time when it had been soft and inviting.

He sighed. It no longer amused him, these glamours and pastimes of Faerie. King Auberon lifted his golden goblet and took a long drink.

"Tasteless," he murmured.

But what was there to do instead? How could he fill his time?

An idea came to him. He could leave this place altogether. Oh, not permanently. Just long enough to stir the blood. A change of scene would do him good.

Since the slaying of the manticore, the ways between the worlds had been opened again. More than a few of the Fair Folk had ventured to Earth, the world of humans. Those who returned spoke most convincingly of the sport offered in that old playground. The fact that some had not returned at all spoke more convincingly still. Why shouldn't Auberon try something new? Perhaps he'd find what he was looking for in that other place— something to fill this emptiness, these endless days. Something for this heart that currently had no reason to beat other than to keep him alive.

*Yes*, Auberon thought, standing and stretching his long legs. *I will go on an adventure. Remind myself I'm alive.*

Ignoring the calls of his courtiers, he strode across the lawn into the woods. He caught a glimpse of Titania's perplexed face as he passed her without a word. She didn't stop dancing, however, he noted.

Maybe if he vanished she would finally take

notice of him. Maybe she would even miss him.

Through the woods, past the lake, along the stream, all the time thinking. Did Titania wonder why he walked away from her fete? Not that he cared. Oh no, not he.

He walked faster. There was a pleasant place he recalled from the time when the worlds commingled. A simmering little stew of a fair town, a bowshot from London's fortified walls. He remembered it well, a smile crossing his blue face. Who would not? It was a bustling market town when he was there last. Fair Folk like himself traveled there whenever they wanted to; his strange looks were not surprising or out of place to the market people.

He recalled the echoing cries: "What do ye lack? What will ye buy?" Anything that could be bought or bartered was available: spiced ale, porpoise tongues, fine English woolens. Even bears for baiting could be had, and fresh cherries, tart and sweet.

And more. Auberon remembered his purse overflowing with acorns, grass, and leaves, all turning to fairy gold when he wanted it, only to return to its natural state when he left the marketplace. He grinned, thinking of the confusion that transformation must have caused after his departure.

*Let Titania and her minstrels pluck and strum to their hearts' content*, he thought. *I will divert myself with livelier music, and perhaps find a more contented heart for myself there.*

He came to a place of deep quiet. Here the grass grew in a spiral; and beginning at the outermost point, he walked the pattern, whispering the words. He released the magic into the atmosphere and felt himself vanish. He rematerialized in another world.

The first thing he noticed was the smell. Acrid and dirty, the air was something he could taste, and nearly see.

A clattering behind him caused him to turn. To his surprise, a bright white unicorn stood on the broken pavement, looking as out of place as Auberon felt. *The creature must have followed me through the portal*, Auberon surmised. Before he could approach the beautiful animal, it whinnied, shook its pure white mane, and trotted away. *Odd*, Auberon thought. It almost seemed as if the unicorn had a destination in mind. *Unlike me.*

King Auberon turned back to survey his surroundings. What had happened to his fair town? He recognized the shape of the coast; the docks jutted out into the water in the same locations as they had all those years ago. But now the piers were rotting, the water was coated with slick oil, and even the birds that circled for food seemed thuggish and menacing.

The sky here, in this other world, was not blue. It was steel gray, speckled with sooty clouds. Tall chimney stacks belched black smoke. For the first time in his long life, Auberon coughed. The polluted atmosphere burned the back of his throat and his green eyes watered.

While his delicate system responded to the particle-laden atmosphere, his pointed ears were assaulted by a jumbled cacophony. The sounds competed with one another to claim title to the most grating. Screeching machinery, constant honking, shouts, and slams made Auberon wonder if the inhabitants had found a way to grow deaf in self-defense. This was a world of chatter and blare.

And it was almost unbearably ugly. After the lush and gilded Faerie, the scene before him was an affront. Filth coated the uneven pavement and buildings. Sharp and jagged lines cut into the gray sky—monstrosities of steel rose up around him. There was nothing soft and welcoming here. All was cold metal.

Once, Auberon had enjoyed the human world's contrast with his pastel Faerie. The edgy energy, the sharp lines, the primitive, less-refined elements—including the inhabitants—had been refreshing, bracing. But this? He looked around. What could this world offer a gentleman such as he? If he took these surroundings as evidence, he and the humans had grown much too far apart. The differences between them were too extreme. He could not imagine finding pleasure in this sad and angry place.

But he had come for adventure; he would not turn tail and run so hastily. Perhaps this sorry spot was merely the ragged outskirts of a less desolate town. *I shall search deeper in*, he decided. *Perhaps that's precisely what the unicorn was doing—perhaps it has been here before.*

Auberon left the wharves, turning his back on the oil-slicked water. Just a few yards ahead he spotted a thick-necked man in a stained shirt and trousers talking to a young woman. It was the woman who truly caught Auberon's attention. Not just because she had a pretty face and lovely golden hair trailing down her back. It was her garb. She wore the long dress and laced chemise of the market women he had met in the earlier days. Was she a visitor like himself? He slipped into an alleyway to listen, curious if he would even understand their language anymore.

"So, you slip your soul in here," the young woman explained to the slovenly man, holding up a glass sphere. "Then you've got it, darling. Your own world. Any way you like it."

The man rubbed his three-day growth of beard. "I don't know, angel. I got a VCR and a wide-screen TV back at my flat. I've got all the entertainment I need, without any highfalutin nonsense about souls." He snorted. "Crystal balls and souls! You actually believe this hooey?"

The woman frowned. "I can't abide a man who laughs at me. I swear I can't."

"Tell you what, angel." He stepped closer to the woman. "Why don't you come back to my place and give me a demo?" He chucked her under the chin. "You don't expect me to buy something sight unseen, do you? I think I ought to get a sample."

The woman jerked her face away from the man. "I expect you'd like to sample me if I gave you half a chance. Which I will not!"

"Awww, be nice, girlie," the man wheedled. "You and me was getting along just fine." He reached for her again, and Auberon had had enough. He stepped out of the shadows and clamped his large blue hand on the man's arm.

"My lady," Auberon said. "Does this churl trouble you?"

The man gaped up at the seven-foot King with the ram's horns on his head, pointed ears, long green hair, and blue skin. His mouth opened and closed several times, and his eyes rolled up into his head. Auberon sensed the man was about to faint, and released him. The man slid to the pavement. Auberon stepped over him. "I believe he will bother you no more."

The woman stared at Auberon, and blinked several times. Then she cast her eyes downward and curtsied.

"Goodness me, a gentleman!"

Auberon smiled and tipped his head. "Your servant, lady." Her quick acceptance of his unusual appearance made him suspect that she had seen his like before. Given her clothing and her manner of speech, he wondered if she had somehow visited the old market days when Faerie folk easily passed between the worlds.

"Oh no, your lordship. Begging your pardon, if there's serving to be done here, I'll do it."

"Tell me, if you will, why grace and beauty such as yours are wasted in so desolate a place?"

"Lordship, I sell my globes where I can." She held up a sparkling translucent ball, much like the kind Auberon had seen Gypsy women use to read fortunes at the marketplace. "It's horrid places like this where I find buyers for what I have to sell. Precious few decent people believe in paradise nowadays. And most of those think they've already bought their piece of it."

Auberon held out his hand. She put the globe

in his blue palm. "This is paradise? This bauble?" He tried to hide a smile.

The woman's irritated expression indicated that his efforts to conceal his disbelief had not worked. "Pardon me, lordship. But when I say apples I don't mean oranges. Try it and then tell me it's not paradise." Her chin jutted out in challenge.

"I am Auberon of the Fay, lady," Auberon declared. "I have ruled a realm of high Magick longer than your upstart race has sported thumbs. Shall a lord of Faerie trust his soul to a toy of man's devising? I think not."

The woman's manner completely changed. She slumped and lowered her eyes. "Of course a gentleman of your quality couldn't lower himself," she said apologetically. She curtsied again. "I beg your pardon, my lord. It's just that you were so kind to me, I had hoped that . . ." She stopped herself and shook her head. "No . . . no . . . I shan't speak of hope today. It's as you say. You belong on a throne and my place is in the gutter."

"Lady, you take my words too much to heart," Auberon protested. He didn't want to offend her; he didn't want her to leave. He enjoyed her spunky defiance, her pretty face, her familiar language. He liked the attention and the unpredictability of a simple flirtation—a game without consequences. "Tell me your name, lady."

"Gwendolyn," she replied in a meek voice.

"Now, my Gwendolyn, let us remain friends. Shall so slight a grievance part us? I would not have you think I scorn you or your race and its achievements."

She seemed eager to part ways, as if she were still wounded by the slight. She held out her pretty little hand. "Please, lordship, give me the globe. I really must go."

"You doubt me and my sincerity. How shall I make it up to you?" He studied the globe and noticed it had holes in its top and its bottom for a person to insert his fingers. "Look, I'll try out your little bauble if it will make you feel better."

Her face lit up with delight. Auberon gave the girl a grin, pleased that he had soothed her ruffled feelings. She really was most attractive. Throwing caution to the winds, he plunged his fingers into the holes.

"Arghghh!" He threw his head back and wailed. A great whooshing surged though his entire body, as if he were being flooded from the inside out. He tried to extract his fingers, but they were locked in somehow. He struggled against the pull of the globe; he felt the evil object draining something vital from him—more vital even than blood. In his final moments of self-awareness, he realized this was not a means of finding paradise. It was a device to trap souls. Then the world turned even more colorless, and Auberon felt nothing at all.

A sly grin crossed Gwendolyn's face. "Thank you, Lovey-horns, that was such a gallant gesture. I knew from the moment I saw you you were a perfect gentleman. Now let me take you away from all this."

# Chapter Four

TIM LEFT THE ABANDONED LOT in a hurry, heading for Molly's house. "Who would have ever thought imaginary friends could turn real?" he wondered. Tim shuddered.

*Even thoughts have consequences*, he realized. The Wobbly started out as scraps and sticks—now he'd become a full-blown predator. "How could I have known?" Tim said. "I was just five years old when I made him." He certainly never imagined he'd have to rescue one set of imaginary friends from another!

He grinned. Tanger and Crimple were awfully cute. He liked meeting them in the . . . well, *flesh* didn't exactly seem the right word, since they were made of twigs. Anyway, he'd gone to the lot to come up with evidence for Molly that he truly did magic. Tanger and Crimple were certainly that! Only once again, Tim couldn't be certain how that trick had been accomplished. The creatures just seemed to have happened.

*Happened because magic happened*, Tim thought. What had they all called him? The Opener. And the Wobbly had said that Tim had "opened the way." *I do seem to have a knack for opening up paths between worlds*, Tim thought. *I've been back and forth between several already.*

*I'll worry about the significance of all this later*, Tim told himself. *Right now, I have bigger things to worry about—like keeping Molly waiting.*

Tim arrived at Molly's street. The monumental nature of what he was about to tell her slowed him down. Truth be told, he was also kind of nervous about seeing her, because he was now over an hour late. "So this is how Clint Eastwood felt in all those high noon–showdown sort of movies," he muttered nervously. "No wonder he moved so slowly." It was only then that he realized he was now walking. He smacked his forehead. "Doofus," he said. "You left your skateboard back at the lot! And there's no time to go get it now." Well, maybe the Narls would look after it for him. He'd stop by and retrieve it later.

Tim knocked on the door. He heard the sound of bolts being drawn back. Molly opened the door just a smidge, leaving the chain lock in place.

"Oh, it's you," she said disdainfully.

"Uh, sorry I'm late," Tim said. "It's just . . . something came up. Quite unexpected."

"Uh-huh." Molly peered at him through the sliver of opened door. "And I should forgive you . . . why?"

"Because . . . because . . ." Tim stuck his hands in his pockets, fiddling with his change. "Because I'm super sorry? Extra sorry, stupendously, stratospherically sorry?"

Molly grinned. "Now that's more like it."

Tim grinned back. "Brilliant."

Molly shut the door again so that she could undo the chain. She flung it open, and Tim saw that she'd had her coat on all along. "I'm going out," she hollered back into the house, then shut the door behind her.

"Okay," she declared. "You're going to take me out for ice cream now like you promised."

That was news to Tim. "I did?"

Molly raised one eyebrow.

"Of course I did," Tim said hastily.

Molly seized his hand, dragging him down the walkway. "We need to make a quick getaway. Otherwise we'll be joined by the entire clan."

Molly came from a large family, and there always seemed to be spare uncles or cousins or aunties around.

"So, you said there was something you

wanted to talk to me about," Molly said as they rounded the corner.

"Er, yes."

Tim kept his eyes fixed on his sneakers. One step, another step. Each step he took was one more taken without telling Molly his big secret. *Okay*, he told himself. *The next step and you'll spill everything. Ooops. There went another three steps. Okay, at the next traffic signal I'll stop and say—*

"Hold on!" he heard Molly call behind him. "Where do you think you're going?"

Tim stopped and turned around. He had been so focused on his feet, and the words going around in his head, that he hadn't noticed that he'd lost Molly. She stood at the bottom of the steps of a building that had a sign hanging out front.

"Swan Dance School?" Tim asked, walking back and reading the sign. "What sort of ice cream are you expecting to find here? Nutcracker Ripple? Swan Lake Surprise?"

Molly put her hands on her hips and rolled her eyes. "We're not getting ice cream here, dodo. I'm just picking up my knapsack and stuff. I spaced after lessons and left it in my locker."

"You take dance lessons?" Tim was astonished. "But you don't look like . . . I mean, uhm . . ." He trailed off, knowing that he had already said the wrong thing. He tried again. "I mean, I never would have guessed that you—"

"Oh, be quiet," Molly cut him off. "You'll only get yourself in deeper if you keep on."

Tim shoved his hands in his pockets again and said nothing.

"There's a lot you don't know about me, Timothy Hunter," Molly declared. "So there!" With that, she twirled around, clomped up the stairs in her heavy boots, and went inside.

"And there's a lot you don't know about me, Molly O'Reilly." Tim sank onto the step to wait. He let out a frustrated sigh. *Am I ever going to be able to talk without putting my foot in it? Girls are just too confusing.* He shook his head. *Maybe I ought to be a monk—the ones who take a nice vow of silence. Then maybe I wouldn't get into so much trouble.*

Molly dashed up the stairs to her locker, but instead of opening it, she leaned against it, hugging herself. She felt giddy and full of energy. She giggled—and that was something she rarely did. "He's so cute when he's embarrassed," she said happily to herself.

"Is someone there?" a voice called from the studio.

Molly glanced into the room that she had thought was empty. A beautiful red-haired girl, a little older than Molly, was stretching at the barre.

"I should have known," Molly called to Marya. "Don't you ever stop?"

Marya did several grand jetés to cross the room, and stood in the doorway. "Of course I do. When Annie comes to fetch me or the janitor locks me out."

Molly knew that Annie was Marya's guardian. But Molly didn't know what had happened to Marya's parents and didn't think it would be polite to ask. Annie worked long hours as a waitress, which meant Marya could spend loads of time at the dance studio.

"What are you doing here?" Marya asked.

Molly rummaged in her locker and found the books she needed for school. She shoved them into her knapsack. "Just getting my stuff. I would have left them till tomorrow, but we've got an exam coming up. Industrial revolution."

"I've heard of that," Marya said. "It wasn't much fun if I remember. Or maybe that was some other revolution."

Molly looked at Marya oddly. She liked the girl—Marya was far and away the best student at Miss Swan's, but she never acted stuck-up or snotty like some of the other advanced girls. But there was no denying that she was very strange. There were all sorts of things that Marya didn't know, and the things that she did know were awfully peculiar. Molly always assumed that was because Marya came from some other country. It wasn't Marya who told her that; it was Marya's accent. The red-haired girl never talked about herself.

There was something a little fragile about Marya that made Molly not want to pry. But she wished she could get to know her better.

"Say," Molly said. "Do you want to come have ice cream with me and my boyfriend? He's waiting downstairs."

Marya's face brightened. "I would love to!"

She looked so happy that Molly was glad she had asked. Maybe Marya was lonely and that was why she danced so much. But Molly knew it was also because Marya loved to dance in a way she couldn't quite grasp. Sure, Molly enjoyed the classes well enough, but she was taking them more to please her mum than anything else. Give her a good rugby scrimmage and lots of races and Molly would be content. With Marya, it was different. Marya seemed more alive when she danced; something shone out of her as she moved.

Molly hovered in the doorway as Marya untied her pink satin pointe shoes and put them into her little dance bag. She changed into thick socks and sneakers, grabbed her coat, and slung her bag over her shoulder. "Ready," Marya said.

They headed down the stairs, Molly's boots making loud clomping sounds, Marya's sneakers softly padding beside them.

"Oh, listen," Molly cautioned. "When you meet my boyfriend, don't let on that you know he's my boyfriend, all right? He gets embarrassed about the silliest things."

"Boys are so strange," Marya commented. "They—well, you just never know how they'll react to things."

Molly eyed her curiously. Clearly Marya was talking about one boy in particular, but Molly would never intrude unless invited.

Out on the stoop, Tim rummaged in his pockets, feeling for change. He hadn't planned on an ice cream expedition. "Next time I have to buy ice cream I hope I'll get *some* advance warning," he muttered. He pulled his hand out and stared down at the coins. "I've got almost enough here for a thimbleful of Rocky Road."

He heard the door open above him. "I'm back," Molly announced. "And I brought a friend."

"Uh, Molly, I don't know how to tell you this . . ." He stood and turned around.

Shock made him stumble backward. The girl with Molly—he knew her! But it was impossible for her to be here. She had come from another world entirely. In fact, she was the reason he had gone to Free Country. But here she was, large as life, standing right in front of him. With Molly! They even seemed to know each other. Molly had called her a "friend."

The red-haired girl looked equally stunned, but seeing Timothy was clearly a happy surprise for her. With great excitement she turned to Molly and said, "Molly! You never told me your boyfriend was a magician!"

Tim felt his entire body grow cold for an instant, then flush so hot that sweat beaded up on his forehead. He knew his face must be beet red, and the tips of his ears burned.

Did Marya actually just tell Molly that he was a magician? Man! He'd spent the last several hours trying to work up the nerve to explain it to Molly in exactly the right way and here Marya blurted it out just like that. And, hang on, there was that other word in there that he was having trouble processing. _Boyfriend_. Yeah, that was it. If he was Molly's boyfriend, wouldn't he have known about it? He wasn't _that_ daft. But the only way Marya would have thought he was Molly's boyfriend was if Molly had said so herself, which meant . . . which meant _what_?

As Tim tried desperately to get words to form, Molly looked back and forth between Tim and

Marya. "You two know each other?" Then she shook her head sharply as if something had just woken up inside her brain. "Wait a minute—a magician?"

"Oh yes!" Marya exclaimed. "I never would have found this wonderful world if I hadn't been sent from Free Country to find Timothy." She turned to Tim. "What happened? Is Free Country okay?"

Even if Tim had been capable of speech at that moment, he would never have had the chance to answer. Both girls began firing questions at him.

"Magician like Zatanna on telly or magic like wizards and real spells and things?" Molly demanded.

"How did you get back from Free Country?" Marya asked.

"What is she talking about?" Molly asked. "Where is Free Country?"

"Is everyone there all right?" Marya asked.

"When did you go out of town? Why didn't I know about it?"

"Uh—uh—uh . . ." Tim managed to say. The two girls' curiosity and demands for explanations felt like an actual force pushing him backward. The faster he backed up, the quicker they moved.

He turned and dashed into an alley, but their questions still pursued him.

"Wait, Tim!" Molly called.

"Why didn't you tell Molly about being a magician? Is it a secret?"

"What else are you keeping from me?"

Tim came to a dead end. He whirled around. They were charging toward him.

Panic threw Tim's hands up out in front of him like a traffic guard signaling stop. "Just stop! Let me think!" he cried.

The girls did stop. Completely.

Marya had one foot up, ready to take another step. Molly's elbows were bent to help her gain speed. Their mouths were open, mid-sentence. Tim had magically frozen them. And he had no idea how he'd done it.

# Chapter Five

DANIEL HUDDLED ON THE STEPS beneath a statue in Piccadilly Circus and rubbed his sore, dirty foot. The stone was cold, but at least he could rest without being noticed up here.

*London is right strange*, he thought. *It's all been changed while I was in Free Country*. Sure, he had been back a few times on missions, but he never stayed long, and he had kept mostly to the outskirts in order to attract less attention. He had seen on those trips that the clothing people wore was different, and the vehicles on the streets, but it never occurred to him that the entire city itself would be nearly unrecognizable to him.

There was a time he could slip around the shadows, never being noticed unless he had it in his mind to be. Now he stood out, and got caught in the stares of the crowds. Had there been this many people out strolling in the streets back in his own time? Mind, he'd lived a crowded existence back then. Five to a room, ten to a flat. The work crews in the factory were in the dozens, all eating, sweating, cursing, working, almost as if they'd been chained together. But surely not so many people walked through the center of town then.

"Aye me," he groaned, switching to rubbing his other foot. He'd been all over London for days, and nights, too, looking for Tim or Marya, and he was beginning to lose hope. Perhaps this had been a bad idea, coming here. He'd gone soft by being in Free Country, and this city was hard. This adventure was one he would have wanted to run by Marya before undertaking. Talking to Marya always had helped him get his thoughts straight. But that right there was the problem. No Marya. So he'd come to London to find her, and he'd failed.

*This London is too strange*, he thought. *I don't know my way 'round no more.* He felt a lump thicken in his throat as he thought he might never see Marya again.

He bent over, resting his elbows on his knees and his face in his filthy hands. He breathed hard, trying not to cry. *It is dreadful hard on a cove to lose a girl this way*, he thought. *Not knowing where she'd got to. Or if she were all right, even.*

"Not that Marya was truly my girl," he said out loud. She'd have laughed herself blue if he'd ever gone and called her that. Lord, how she would have laughed. He laughed, too, imagining her twirling around like she did, propelled by her laughter, and him not minding that it was him she was laughing at. Then his laugh caught in his throat as he realized that the picture he had in his imagination would never come true again.

Another thought squeezed its way into his mind. Marya would be growing up now. Free Country stopped all that—while there, you stayed the age you were when you arrived. *It gives a cove the staggers*, he thought. Marya being all grown up into a real lady and still being his Marya on the inside. *Come to think of it, if I stays here, that's going to be my fate, too. I'll need to be making up my mind soon.* Another thing he wished he could talk to Marya about.

He wiped his nose on his ragged sleeve, donned his battered top hat and leaped down onto the pavement. If anybody could figure this rum place out and make it sit up and do tricks for her, Marya could. Yeah, she was all right; he was certain of it. It was himself he had to start worrying about now. Himself and his revenge on Timothy Hunter.

"Ow!" A sharp knock on the side and in the

knee caught him smartly and sent him sprawling.

Three well-dressed gentlemen carrying leather cases had banged right into him. "Beg your pardon," a tweedy voice said. But did they stop? Not even. They knocked him over and kept walking.

"Used to be it was walking sticks the swells would thrash you with, when you was in their way," Daniel grumbled as he stood up. He dusted himself off, then gave up once he realized how dirty his jacket had become.

He passed by a shop window and glared at the mannequins. "Drat you suit people," Daniel cursed. "You took it. You took our place from us. Now there's nowhere for people like us to go."

He glanced down and saw a grate in the pavement. "You ain't left us nothing. Not a drop of ale nor crust of bread. Nor a spark of fire to warm our hands at." He undid his belt and wrapped it around the iron grate. He tugged it, making sure it was tight. "But you can't have changed everything!" With a sharp pull, he yanked the grate out of the sidewalk. He fell backward as it came loose, and landed on his rear. He clambered back up onto his hands and knees and peered down into the dark opening. A smile slowly spread across his face.

"There's got to be someplace them suitcase

blokes ain't got round to spoiling yet. Somewhere something's got to be the same." He lowered himself down, and landed with a splash in the sewer under the sidewalk.

The water was warmish and thick. He was used to discomfort, or he had been before he found refuge in Free Country. It would just take some getting used to again.

He fiddled in his pockets and pulled out a matchbox and a candle. "Clever me," he congratulated himself. *Wise to be prepared.* He struck the match and lit the candle, illuminating the tunnel.

The stink didn't bother him: It was finally something familiar. "Here's one place them fancy types hasn't spoiled," Daniel muttered. He'd spent hours, days even, down here in the old times. They were good hiding places then. And for the first time he'd found something in London that hadn't changed.

*Wonder if anybody works the old drains nowadays. Must be all kinds of things what runs down from that dismal shiny place up there. Wouldn't be surprised if the pickings were better now than in the old days. That lot up there, they looked to be the sort of wasters as would be losing things left and right.*

Daniel wandered in the gloom, remembering the old days, the old gang. Old Barmy Barney who told a great tale. Ragtag Mary. The Fire King who had introduced him to the tunnels; they were a good place for a boy to hide after picking a pocket or angering one's master. The Fire King knew all the scavenger's trades, but Daniel liked it best when he could watch the young man eat fire. An uncommon ratcatcher he was, too. *What's become of him?* Daniel wondered. *It'd be worth a penny to see him again. All of them. But of course, they'd have died a long time ago*, Daniel reminded himself.

He suddenly noticed something. The water was rising quickly. *Better hightail it out of here for now.* He held up the candle and discovered that the closest exit had been bricked up. "They have been down here, too," he gasped. The water reached his waist now. He held the candle up high, but it fizzled out, and he was left in the darkness.

"Help!" he cried. He hoped against hope that someone would be down here. "Help me!"

He felt a pair of hands clamped over his eyes. "You took your time about calling, didn't you, my Daniel?" a familiar voice rasped in the darkness. "You always were the shy one."

That voice. Daniel felt a shiver as he recognized the speaker. It couldn't be—could it? "Reverend Slaggingham?" Daniel blurted. "Can it possibly be you?"

"Can and is, my lad!"

The tall old man with the silvery muttonchop whiskers released Daniel. A moment later the tunnel was illuminated again. Slaggingham had produced a lantern and lit it with a flourish.

"So you do remember me." Slaggingham squinted at Daniel with narrow steel-gray eyes, his pasty face lined with the same wrinkles he'd always had. "Not too kindly, I see. Well, I've come down in the world since you knew me as the head of your old orphanage, Danny. And it changed me. I'm a different man. Transformed, as it were."

"But how—" Daniel couldn't understand how Slaggingham could still be around. Daniel wasn't too good with sums, and he knew time did funny things in Free Country, but Slaggingham had already been old when Daniel had lived in the Bad World. That was a long, long time ago. Daniel could tell that from his quick missions to the Bad World from Free Country and from the way the newcomers looked and spoke when they arrived.

If Slaggingham understood Daniel's unformed question, he ignored it. He also seemed to simply accept that Daniel hadn't died—or aged—in the long years since they'd seen each other. *Well, if he's not asking, I'm not telling*, Daniel decided.

"Welcome to our humble nest, little brother,"

Slaggingham rasped. "You couldn't have come at a better time."

"That so?" Daniel had never quite trusted Slaggingham, as he'd seen him go from kindly to enraged in the middle of a sentence; so the old gent's interest in him made him feel a bit dubious.

"You've been lost awhile, haven't you? Been treated rough, too, I shouldn't wonder. Well, there's nothing like being kicked about to give a chap a healthy appetite, I always say."

"Is that what you always say?" Daniel asked, hoping Slaggingham wouldn't clip him one for impertinence. It was the sort of cheek that had landed Daniel in trouble with the reverend in the past.

"Would you fancy a spot of tea before we put those clever hands of yours to work?" Slaggingham asked. "I was just on my way to the factory."

So that was it. Slaggingham was going to put him back on the assembly line. In the old days, it was Reverend Slaggingham who set the boys to work, farming them out at tender ages to other masters and then collecting their wages, tossing them the spare penny as recompense. Well, Daniel would make up his own mind about that. But much as he hated to admit it, it was nice to be with someone he knew. After so much that was new and unfamiliar, it was a relief to look upon a familiar face—and one that was much friendlier now than it had ever been before. And he could sure use that tea. He'd had so little to eat since leaving Free Country.

Without Daniel even noticing, Slaggingham had been walking him along the tunnels, Daniel now realized. He could see light streaming from an archway up ahead. Sounds, too, were echoing around the tunnels—clanging and whirring and clanking, just like the old days.

"Ah, here we are," Slaggingham announced. They stood in the archway, and Daniel gaped at the sight.

In this part of the tunnels the ceiling was high and vaulted, higher than the clubhouse tree back in Free Country, higher than the houses along the quiet, tree-lined street where Daniel had walked earlier that day. In the center loomed a tall monster of a machine. Valves, gauges, and dials whirred, while wires sizzled and smoke rose around it. Metal scaffolding allowed workers to reach out with long metal sticks to manipulate levers and to poke at cinders.

Daniel watched the workers for a bit. They were a mixed lot—mostly men, but from their clothing they seemed to range from rich to poor, and the many styles indicated they came from different time periods. *Sort of like Free Country*, Daniel observed. In Free Country, kids came in wearing whatever they had on, whether it was medieval tunics or blue jeans.

*Only there don't seem to be much "free" about these blokes*, Daniel thought. They moved in rhythmic patterns, as if they were part of the machinery itself. Only the ones in charge, like Slaggingham, and a man the reverend greeted in passing as Brother Salamander, seemed to have any life to them. The rest were silent drones.

*No way am I becoming one of them lot*, Daniel vowed silently.

"Isn't it a beauty?" Slaggingham rested his arm lightly on Daniel's shoulder. The reverend still towered over him, as he always had, but Daniel noticed his touch was gentler.

*Perhaps old Slaggingham is a new man, sure enough*, Daniel thought. *He ain't calling me a "foul heathen" now. And he ain't raised a hand to me once, much less a stick. He don't whiff of rum like he used to, neither. Now he smells like grease and oil, like you'd get working with machines.*

"It's a treat to have you here, lad," Slaggingham said. "To be able to square things with you at last."

"What do you mean, square things?"

"Wasn't I bad to you back in the old days?

Didn't I bully you, thrash you, and call you names?"

"You did." Daniel shrugged. "But so did every other cove with a pocketful of bills. Compared to some others, what you done was nothing. You never shoved me down no chimneys to get scraped raw as meat. You never soused me with pig's brine when I came out bloody. You never starved me to keep me willing to work."

"Stop," Slaggingham moaned. He patted his chest. "You're wrenching my heart, lad." He reached out suddenly and pulled Daniel into an awkward embrace. Then he held the boy out at arm's length and bent down so they were eye to eye. "I was going to take you on at the factory," Slaggingham confided. "Make you an extractor operative grade one. But I know you better now. You've fire in your eyes, my boy, and steel in your heart." He waggled a finger in front of Daniel's face. "I want you to be my partner, young man." He stood straight up again and shot out his hand. "Give us a shake on it."

Daniel hesitated. For all of Slaggingham's big act, he still didn't trust him. Besides, Slaggingham had never done anything that didn't serve himself best, no matter the consequences for the other bloke. "What precisely is an extractor operative? What is it that you are planning to extract?" He hoped it wasn't teeth.

A whistle sounded and the silent workers moved from one part of the machinery to another.

Slaggingham got a glint in his eyes, and he grinned broadly. He stuck his thumbs in his suspenders and his chest expanded like a pigeon's. "Why, happiness!" he crowed. "We will be extracting happiness from those who have too much of it, and giving it to those who have too little. Haven't you noticed that there is an unfair distribution of happiness in this world, lad?"

"True enough," Daniel conceded. It sounded pretty ridiculous to him, but what did he know compared to the old reverend? "How do you plan to be doing the extracting?"

"Ahhhhhhhh, my boy, my boy." Slaggingham rubbed his hands together. "Wait until you feast your eyes on my pride and my joy. My crown jewel of all my stunning creations."

He led Daniel up a metal ladder bolted to the brick wall. This brought them up to a catwalk suspended high above the floor. They clattered along the catwalk and through another archway. Steam and odorous vapors rose from the extensive machinery below them.

In the dim light Daniel could make out silent figures moving in unison around the machine. Daniel was impressed. Slaggingham had a major operation going down here. *And he wants me to be a part of all of it,* Daniel mused. *Me! Like he thinks I'm worth something.*

Slaggingham stood by a control panel built into one of the walls. "Let me adjust the lights so you can better witness the genius of modern times." Slaggingham grabbed a lever and pulled it. It creaked and groaned as he pushed it down, then several lights shorted out.

"Confound and blast it!" Slaggingham smacked the lever in frustration. "It's jammed again!"

"Wants oiling?" Daniel suggested.

"Wants protection." Slaggingham growled. He turned and grabbed one of the lanterns hanging on the wall.

Daniel's eyebrows rose. "Protection from what?"

"Sabotage!" Slaggingham held the lantern out over the railing of the catwalk and scanned the area.

Daniel followed his gaze. He was startled to see a small fellow who seemed to be made entirely of tools disappearing around a corner.

"You!" Slaggingham cried, waving his fist in the air. "You blighter! You will regret this! I shall have you, I shall!"

"Who is that bloke?" Daniel asked, intrigued

by the odd creature's appearance.

"A saboteur. An enemy of progress! Awn the Blink is the tool-fingered troublemaker's name."

"Where did he come from?" Daniel asked. He'd never seen anything like Awn the Blink before. And what a peculiar name. "How did he get down here?"

"He's here because some slurry-brained high-city magic brat used to believe in him. Thanks to his shenanigans we're behind schedule." Slaggingham paced back and forth, muttering oaths and curses.

Daniel's stomach growled. "Didn't you say something about tea?" Daniel asked. "That ain't going off the schedule, is it?"

Slaggingham stopped prowling the catwalk and peered at Daniel. He glanced again in the direction Awn the Blink had vanished, then back at Daniel. "You wouldn't care to inspect the Extractor first?"

Daniel crossed his arms over his chest. "Not a bit of it." He'd been offered a proper tea, by gum, and he was determined to have it.

Slaggingham seemed disappointed, but he shrugged. "I shall tell you more about it over tea then . . . partner?"

Daniel still wasn't sold on the partner idea, so he said nothing.

"Come with me, lad." Slaggingham climbed down the ladder, and walked Daniel around the Extractor. Once more, Daniel wondered about the workers. He couldn't precisely say what was wrong with them—he'd certainly seen dronelike behavior among the factory line workers back in the old days—but they disturbed him anyway.

As they walked, Slaggingham slung an arm across Daniel's shoulders. "There are two kinds of people in the world, Daniel," he said, "the happy ones, curse them, and us. And why is that, I ask you?"

That was a daft question, the answer being so obvious. Daniel ticked off the reasons on his fingers. "They eat regular, and we don't. That's one thing. They has places that belongs to them. And we don't. They ain't got to lurk or drudge like us. And they have *things*. Lots of nice things."

"Jolly good!" Slaggingham acted as though Daniel had aced an exam at school. "That brain of yours is a ticker, my boy. Give *this* a tick then. Slaggingham's law informs us that there's a finite amount of happiness floating around in the world. Finite meaning limited, as you know."

"Yeah, I know that," Daniel muttered. "I ain't stupid."

"Oh, I know, lad. You are indeed the brightest

sweep I have ever known. Now, let's say you wanted to free up some happiness for you and your mates to grab. How would you do it?"

Daniel was stumped. He bit his lip. "I—I don't know," he admitted. It seemed impossible. After all, if folks could do such a thing, wouldn't they all be doing it by now?

"You'd manufacture misery, that's what you'd do!" Slaggingham crowed. "Then you'd sell it to happy people. Which would make them unhappy, of course, as sure as Christmas comes once a year." Slaggingham stopped walking and began gesturing dramatically, illustrating his vision. "When the happiness came trickling out of their punctured hearts, you and your mates would catch every last drop of it with Slaggingham's Anti-Tantalic Extractor Apparatus. Patent pending."

Daniel's head swum. It made no sense, did it? But, coo, wouldn't it be the staggers if it could be done? Be a way to bring those swells down a peg. And he'd be there to swoop in to soak up all that happiness.

"How do you manufacture misery?" Daniel asked. "And why would anyone buy it?"

A grin creaked its way across Slaggingham's craggy face. "That's the easiest part of all. Consumerism. It's the capitalist system. Advertising.

It's been going on for ages. Now we can tap into the existing system and use it to our own purposes."

As appealing as this amazing plan sounded, Daniel didn't think it was something he really wanted to be a part of. There was something wrong in the logic, even if he couldn't put his finger on it or find the words to explain it to the old reverend.

Besides, Slaggingham still hadn't coughed up that tea. Had his offer for refreshment been a sham? *How can you trust a man who not only should have died ages and ages ago but who tantalizes you with a promise of a spot of tea, only to produce nothing? Instead, he walks you about the endless tunnels, through another archway, and to yet another gigantic machine.*

"About that tea—" Daniel began, but Slaggingham cut him off.

"What's this?" Slaggingham demanded. "Why aren't you all at your stations?"

Daniel noticed that here, instead of working busily, the workers were all standing around in a large circle, away from the machine. Tools lay scattered on the floor, as if they had simply dropped them.

"What is going on here?" Slaggingham bellowed.

As the workers registered Slaggingham's voice, the circle slowly opened up.

Slaggingham grabbed Daniel's shoulder with a viselike grip. "Impossible!" he cried.

"Ow!" Daniel yelped.

Slaggingham didn't notice Daniel trying to shake out of his clutches. He was frozen, staring at something straight ahead. Daniel peered through the group and gasped. A unicorn stood gazing up at the happiness-extractor machine.

"Grease and burning gaskets, it can't be!" Slaggingham cried. "A unicorn, drat its shiny hide. Well, get the ridiculous thing out of here."

None of the workers moved. It was as if the unicorn had them all hypnotized.

Daniel stared at the creature and felt his heart flutter. It was beautiful, and hopeful, and had no right to be there amid all their dark squalor. It was too white, too clean; it made him angry. He understood Slaggingham's rage. Seeing it was a reminder of what they were not. Was the thing laughing at them? Did it come here just to make them feel bad about their lot in life?

Slaggingham scanned his workers and must have realized they were useless in this situation. "It's the glue shed for you, you scurvy agitator," he shouted at the unicorn.

With several clicking sounds, Slaggingham popped a strange metal eyepiece into place. Daniel was startled: The weapon seemed to have grown out of Slaggingham's coat. *He's been armed the whole time*, Daniel realized. *Glad I didn't cross him.*

Then, by merely blinking his eye, Slaggingham set off a round of ammunition straight at the animal.

The unicorn reared up and galloped away down one of the branching tunnels. Every single bullet missed its mark. No one made a move to follow the creature.

"Confound you, you popinjay!" Slaggingham bellowed. "You fairy-tale jumping jack! Drat you and that meddling Timothy Hunter!"

Daniel's face grew hot, and his heart thudded double time in his chest. "Did you say . . . did you say Timothy Hunter?" he gasped.

With several clicks, Slaggingham's weapon folded back into his coat. Slaggingham looked down at Daniel. "I did."

"Are you telling me that he's the one who is causing the trouble down here? Stopping work and making little blokes out of tools?"

"That is the villain. Do you know him?"

"I'll say I do. He stole my girl, Marya." Daniel took a deep breath. "If you're against Timothy Hunter, then I'm your man. I hate him."

"So does that mean we have an agreement?" Slaggingham asked eagerly.

Daniel nodded, then thrust out his hand for the man to shake. "We does indeed."

# Chapter Six

TIM STARED AT MOLLY and Marya, both frozen mid-step. He balled his hands into fists, squeezed his eyes shut, and banged his temples.

"You've really done it now, Tim," he admonished himself. He opened his eyes again. Unfortunately the scene in front of him hadn't changed. Proof of his supreme idiocy—as if he needed any further evidence.

"But what exactly *have* I done?" he asked out loud. "And how do I undo it?"

He walked in a slow circle all the way around Molly and Marya. It was as if they were statues in an art museum. They looked completely alive.

"Of course they look alive—they *are* alive!" Tim hated the sound of the terror in his voice. It went all squeaky. He studied them again. "They're just . . . on pause." He fiddled with the junk in his pockets, hoping the familiar action would help him think.

It didn't.

Tim slumped onto the curb, his eyes never leaving Molly. He got into this mess because he freaked out, and instead of facing the situation like a man, like a hero, or maybe like his dad, Tamlin, would have, he just tried to stop it so he could pretend it wasn't happening. Which made everything much worse, because something else happened instead—and he was the one who had done it!

He stood back up again, pacing back and forth in front of the girls. He had wanted to tell Molly himself about the magic; he had even planned a demonstration. But this wasn't quite what he'd had in mind.

He planted himself next to Molly, taking in her sparkling eyes. What was the expression on her face? She seemed excited and urgent. She didn't look angry; that was a relief. Of course, that was before she knew he could freeze her, and might not be able to unfreeze her.

He glanced up and down the street. Luckily, he had ducked into an alley and the girls had followed, so there were no cars, no people, no witnesses. He wondered—if there had been, would they all be frozen, too? He had no idea how wide a range this freezing power had.

He took a deep breath. He was afraid to try to

undo what he'd done because he didn't know how he had done it. What if he made things worse?

But he had to do something. He worried that the longer they were frozen in time, the harder it would be to undo. Or that there would be side effects or something, if they stayed this way too long. And even worse—if he kept Molly out too late her dad would kill them both.

"I've got to quit rabbiting around and get to work," he declared. *Every time I try to play it safe*, he realized, *things turn out worse. Well, there's no one here to help me, so this is up to me to fix.*

He remembered his first real magic, the time he had kept the snow from falling on Kenny, Tamlin's friend. The secret to that had been concentration, focus, relaxation, and will.

He stood in front of the girls. "I'll undo Marya first," he decided. "She'll need less of an explanation. And she can get me up to speed on what Molly already knows."

What had the Trenchcoat Brigade told him? Magic answers need. He needed a moment to think when the girls came after him. He felt it really strongly and it happened. In Free Country, he was angry at being used, and that energy nearly blasted the world apart. What he had to learn was to use his brain, not just his chaotic feelings. That's why the snow trick worked. All right. Focus.

He waved his hands in front of Marya. "Undo!" he declared.

Nothing happened.

"Great," Tim muttered. "Just great."

*Underground London*

Slaggingham clapped his hands. "All right, all right, comrades. The sideshow is over. Back to work. Every last Jack and Jill of you."

Without a murmur or question, the factory workers turned and shambled their way back to their stations.

Slaggingham grinned at Daniel. "Now, I believe we were about to have tea."

*About time*, Daniel thought. *For a while there it looked as if the tea was merely a figment of the reverend's imagination.*

Slaggingham pushed open a door, and ushered Daniel into a small office. A hot plate sat on the counter and shelves lined the walls, full of dented canned goods. It seemed as if Slaggingham had decorated his office with discards and found his supplies in the rubbish.

*No matter*, Daniel decided. *Food is still food, even if the tin it comes in is dented and the label pulled off.* He'd had far worse in his life.

Slaggingham set about getting the tea. "So, that sly dog Hunter stole your girl, did he?"

"She ran off to London to find him and I ain't seen her since," Daniel replied. "Some might not call that stealing, but I ain't such a fool."

Slaggingham placed the cup of tea and a box of dusty biscuits on the table in front of Daniel. "I could do with a spot of refreshment myself," he said.

Daniel's eyes widened in amazement as Slaggingham pulled off the skin on his hands, revealing machinery underneath. What Daniel had thought were fingers were actually metal contraptions.

"You—you took off your skin!" Daniel blurted.

"My *gloves*, Dan," Slaggingham corrected. "Bless you, you can't expect a man to eat while he's got his gloves on."

Slaggingham stuck the tips of his metal fingers into a little box. Daniel heard a crackling, buzzing sound and watched in awe as Slaggingham shuddered, electric current shooting through his body.

Daniel was speechless. He took a sip of tea, his shaking hands rattling the teacup.

*What does it mean?* Daniel wondered. What

had he just witnessed? *It means,* he realized, *that Slaggingham ain't human! How could that have happened?* Of course, it did explain how Slaggingham managed to still be alive and kicking after so many years. *Has he* always *been a machine?* Daniel frowned, puzzled. He must have been human once, Daniel figured. After all, he'd seen the old gent tuck into a steaming plate of stew while the rest of them looked on, hungry as could be. Slaggingham had needed food back then, like any other bloke. So when—and how—did this change take place?

Daniel took another sip of tea, hoping to soothe his rattled nerves. The warmth did make him feel a bit better. After all, being machinery seemed to have brought out the best in Slaggingham. He had served up tea and biscuits and was treating Daniel much more kindly than he ever had in the past.

Slaggingham removed his fingers from the box and slid his false human skin back over his metal extremities. "So then, we've both got reasons for wanting this Timothy Hunter dead," Slaggingham said. "I say we get right to it."

"Dead?" Daniel repeated. "I'm not so sure about that . . ."

"Ah." Slaggingham nodded knowingly. "So

this girl doesn't mean that much to you, then."

"I never said that!" Daniel protested. "You take that back."

Slaggingham grinned. "Settle down, settle down, lad. I meant no disrespect to you or your young lady. I see I was right about that fire inside you."

"You just don't understand, is all," Daniel grumbled.

"Let me amend our little misunderstanding," Slaggingham said. "What can I do to make this up to you? I don't suppose you carry anything of hers with you, do you?"

"I've got a lock of her hair," Daniel admitted. He felt a slight blush rise in his cheeks. He didn't truly want to reveal everything to Slaggingham, but he was curious about where Slaggingham was going with this.

Slaggingham beamed. "Excellent. Would you like to see the angel again? Your Marya? Give me that lock of her hair and you can."

Daniel pulled out the locket that he secretly wore on a chain around his neck. He always took care that it stayed inside his shirt; he didn't want any of the kids in Free Country to razz him. He had found the locket in Marya's tent after she had left, and he wore it as he waited for her to return. But she never did. Once he realized he might never see her again, he had taken all sorts of things from her little tent. He found her hairbrush, and had combed the long stray hairs out of it and tied them together with a ribbon. Marya had once told him her mother had kept a little lock of her baby hair as a keepsake, so why shouldn't he do the same?

He opened the locket and held out the red strands tied with a blue satin ribbon.

Slaggingham took it. "Very good, very good."

He pushed a button on the wall. A hidden panel slid up with a whoosh, revealing a small machine. This one had some kind of viewing screen on top and a little box with a slot at the bottom. Slaggingham pressed some buttons, and the machine kicked into life with a low hum. The screen went light gray, as if illuminated from inside, waiting for a picture to appear. Slaggingham popped the lock of Marya's hair into the slot. "Now we'll get to see what's what, won't we?"

He stood aside, to allow Daniel to step up to the viewing screen. Daniel's heart thip-thumped again. What was going to happen?

An image slowly formed on the screen. A girl, smiling, her arms reaching straight out toward him.

"Marya!" Daniel cried.

"Flutter my valves, but she is an angel, isn't

she?" Slaggingham said.

Daniel looked up at Slaggingham, his eyes shining. "Oh, you done it. That's her, to the life." Happiness he had never experienced before flooded through him. Finding Reverend Slaggingham had been a stroke of good luck. Thanks to the old gent he'd be able to find Marya again. This was a joyous day!

"I never seen her wear that coat before," Daniel commented.

"She must have bought it since she left . . . er, since she came here," Slaggingham said. "This is showing Marya right this very minute."

"Cor." Daniel looked back at the viewing screen. He could tell she was running—her long hair streamed out behind her. "Where is she?" he asked. "What is she doing?"

Slaggingham pressed another button and a slip of paper popped out of the machine. He glanced at it and said, "She's somewhere in East London, sure as gears have teeth. As for what she's doing, let's have a look."

Slaggingham adjusted the machine and the image pulled back, giving them a long view.

"No," Daniel gasped.

There, large as life, was Marya, only now Daniel could see who she was smiling at, who her arms reached for, who she was running toward. It wasn't Daniel.

It was Timothy Hunter.

All her smiles. All her yearning. It was for that magician! And boiling his blood even more was how intently Tim was staring at Marya.

"The smarmy dog!" Daniel shouted. "He's going to catch her and kiss her. Slag me if he ain't." Daniel whirled around and covered his eyes with his arm. "Make it go away," he pleaded, "before my heart bursts." He flung himself across the room and slumped at the table, burying his face in his hands.

Daniel heard a clicking sound behind him. "It's gone, lad," Slaggingham assured him. "You can look up now."

"Look up?" Daniel said into the crook of his arm, his voice choked with emotion. "I'll tell you when I'll be able to hold my head up again. When that four-eyed traitor is cat's meat and I have Marya back."

"Today can be your day," Slaggingham promised. "I'll help you, I shall. I have another invention—a little something I whipped up that may be of use. Come along, lad."

Daniel wiped his face on his sleeve. He didn't want Slaggingham or any of those workers to see that he'd been crying. He stood and was ashamed of how weak his legs felt. He allowed Slaggingham to lead him through the tunnels, oblivious of the twists and turns they were taking. He didn't care where they went, he just stumbled along, pain filling his every pore.

There were no workers in the room Slaggingham took Daniel to. Just a large column-like machine with wires and dials and whatnots.

"Step inside, lad," Slaggingham instructed.

Daniel stepped up to the glass capsule. "What is it?"

"This beauty is an Amalgo-Reductive Persona Potentiator. It made me what I am today. And it can do as much for you. The glory of it is that it takes what's there inside you and makes it more so."

Daniel stared at the invention. "What will it do?"

"It will reduce your pain," Slaggingham explained, "and increase your power to take on the likes of Tim Hunter."

Daniel's eyes widened. "I'm for that!"

"Climb in, partner," Slaggingham wheedled. "And be everything you can be."

Daniel walked up the little steps into the capsule. Slaggingham pressed a button, and a door in the capsule whirred open. Daniel stepped inside. The moment he did, the door whirred shut again.

It was like standing inside a glass chamber. He peered out, trying to see Slaggingham, but he was all distorted through the glass.

Slaggingham took his place at the control panel. "You've got a lot of spirit, lad. Time to let it show. Let 'er rip."

"Let it out, sir? My spirit?" Once again, Slaggingham was making no sense.

"Yes, lad. Every dirty, poisoned rag of it."

# Chapter Seven

TIM CONTINUED STARING AT Molly and Marya. "Okay, so far I've figured out this much," he told the immobile girls. "It has something to do with time. Somehow time moves one way for you and another way for me—and everyone else."

He put his hands on his hips. *Time is weighed down where they are, keeping them still. They're sort of stuck in it. Funny, I've never thought of time as sticky before.*

Tim held out his hands, moving them closer and closer to Marya. *There.* He felt it. The air around her gave him some resistance—it tingled. In a sharp gesture, he plunged his fingers into the slower-moving molecules and yanked what felt like a heavy blanket off Marya.

Marya stumbled forward with such force that she knocked them both over. "Ooof!" Tim grunted.

"Sorry!" Marya giggled and helped Tim to his

feet. He set his glasses back on his nose. "It's so good to see you," she exclaimed. "I've been meaning to visit you but—"

"Marya!" Tim needed her to stop talking. She was acting as if this were the most normal reunion in the world. That was part of the problem, though: They weren't from the same world. *Actually*, Tim realized, *technically we are. All the kids living in Free Country were originally from here, what they call the Bad World.*

Marya took a breath, then began again, words tumbling out of her. "What with exploring and dancing, I just haven't found the time."

"Marya, slow down a minute," Tim said. "I need to do something about Molly."

Marya turned and looked at Molly. "What is wrong with her?"

Tim snorted. "Her *boyfriend* is a magician. And not a very smart one, I'm afraid." He emphasized the *b* word, testing it out. It didn't sound so bad. But shouldn't he have been included in the discussion when that was decided? It seemed like he was the last to know, as usual.

"Do you think you can catch her?" he asked Marya. "She's bound to have some serious momentum going, like you did, and I don't want her to fall over."

"Sure thing."

Marya got into position next to Molly. "Ready."

Tim felt for the sticky sensation in the air that indicated that time had slowed in that spot. He wiggled his fingers and yanked. Molly lunged forward, and Marya grabbed her, as she nearly tipped over.

"Steady now," Marya said, helping Molly find her footing.

Molly turned to stare at Tim, wide-eyed and openmouthed. The moment of truth had arrived.

"Magic?" she said.

"Boyfriend?" he countered.

Molly blushed. For the first time in his life, Tim had one-upped her.

She gazed down at her clunky boots. "Uh."

"Boyfriend," he repeated. This time, though, it was more of a statement than a question.

Molly laughed. "Well, you had to find out sooner or later. I was hoping that you would work it out yourself."

"Who, me?" Tim's eyebrows rose. "You know me better than that. I don't notice that it's raining until my glasses fog up."

"Hm." Molly took a step closer to him. "Well, I see that you stopped running away, at least."

"I guess I have." He took a step closer to her.

"Does that mean you . . . uh . . . ." She trailed

off and gazed at her feet again.

*Astounding*, Tim thought. *Molly O'Reilly—speechless.*

He decided to not prolong her discomfort. "Yeah, I guess it does." He smiled at her.

Only now it was Molly who backed up. Had he already done something wrong?

She studied his face. "Marya wasn't joking, was she? You are a magician?"

She didn't seem afraid, just curious and amazed.

"Uh, yeah, that's true," he replied. This was going a lot better than he had imagined.

"Wow," she murmured. Then her eyes widened. "Wow!" she cried.

"Yeah, it *is* pretty exciting," Tim admitted.

Molly shoved him aside. "It's beautiful!"

Tim turned to see what had distracted Molly, since she was no longer paying any attention to him. His mouth dropped open.

A white unicorn trotted down the alley toward them.

"What are you doing here?" Tim asked the unicorn. He remembered it from the time he had saved Faerie. Tim and the unicorn had defeated the evil manticore together, and while Tim lay dying the unicorn had kept him company.

*Okay, things are going from weird to weirder.*

*First Marya arrives in my world, now the unicorn? What next?* The worlds were all spilling over into each other. *Maybe I am some kind of Opener after all.*

Tim blinked behind his glasses. Dark, heavy dust was suddenly swirling along the alley. Marya and Molly began to cough.

"Where is it all coming from?" Molly asked.

"What is it?" Tim wondered.

"Is there a fire nearby?"

"I think it's soot," Marya choked out. "You know, like from chimneys."

"There's no wind," Tim observed. "Why is it blowing around so much?"

"It's not blowing around," Molly cried. "It's heading straight toward us."

In moments, Tim, Marya, and Molly were engulfed in the black cloud. The soot and smoke swirled all around them, blocking out the buildings, making them unable to see past a few inches in front of them.

"Let's get out of here." Molly coughed. "I can't see anything!"

"What about the unicorn?" Marya asked.

"If he's as smart as I think he is, he's already gone," Tim assured them.

"No, he's not!" Molly cried. "Look!"

The wind had shifted, making a small break in the soot so they could see. The unicorn, overcome by the fumes and choking on the dirt, sank slowly to the ground.

A harsh voice came out of the black cloud. "I'll say the freakish horsie is gone, you mongrel. And slag me if you ain't a going next!"

Squinting against the nasty air, his eyes tearing, Tim could just make out a figure looming over the fallen unicorn. It was a boy about his age, wearing tattered, old-fashioned clothing and carrying a dingy old broom.

"Daniel?" Marya gasped. "Is that you?"

# Chapter Eight

*Underneath London*

GWENDOLYN LED THE BLUE gentleman through a tunnel filled with water up to their ankles. He was so tall—easily seven feet by Gwendolyn's estimation—that she worried he might scrape those ram's horns he sported on his head against the ceiling in some of the tighter passageways.

"You'll like working for Slaggingham, Loveyhorns," she explained as they slogged through the muck. "He'll give you room and board. Just think, after you've been on the job awhile, you'll even find calluses on those dainty blue hands."

The gentleman never said a word. They rarely did, once their souls had been sucked away. Gwendolyn saw the value in Slaggingham's system; being soulless certainly kept the workers in line. They never once thought of escape, of fighting back. They never once *thought*—only did what they were told to do. They followed orders, these captives, and never questioned, not one little bit.

Sometimes Gwendolyn wondered how Slaggingham had decided which of his merry band to keep and which to discard. She recognized her value—she was bait, pure and simple. But why had Slaggingham dosed her and Brother Salamander with the longevity tonic but not poor old Teddy? Teddy, who had once been known as the Fire King, had become one of the soulless drones, when once he had been among the same rabble-rousing pack of schemers as the luckier ones, like her.

*But* are *we the lucky ones?* The revolution long promised by the reverend had failed to materialize. And they'd been at this for so long.

Gwendolyn cast a glance back at her most recent prize. He was quite the catch—a gentleman! A king, no less, if the elegant blue giant were to be believed. He kindled dim memories, from so long ago that they had the unreality of a dream. He brought to mind market days, before things went so horribly wrong for Gwendolyn and her family, before they lost their farm and their home. She thought she could remember those happy days at the town fair, when she was a wee lass, and creatures of all description ventured to the fair. Gwendolyn had always put those images down to childhood fancy. Seeing this Auberon, this Lovey-horns, made her doubt her doubts.

"It's not as though you're the first king to be captured by the likes of me," Gwendolyn said. "Are you keen on history, dear? It repeats itself, you know. Go back as far as you like. There's always something to be learned. Take the ancient Romans, for instance. Some of those gents could really tell you what was what. I expect you've learned a great deal today, lordship. I hope it hasn't left you too shaken for one tiny lesson more: how to work as though your royal life depended on it. Which, of course, it does."

They had arrived at the middle of a metal catwalk, high above the rising steam of an enormous machine clanging and whirring below them.

Gwendolyn leaned over the metal railings. "Hey, Brother Salamander," she called down to a thin, balding man who was staring at a large clock. "Where's the good reverend got to?"

The thin man looked up. "Don't know, sister. He's forty-nine seconds late for inspection, believe it or not. You might try the commissary. Or his office."

"Hear that, Lovey-horns? You're in luck. You may get a morsel to eat before you're set to drudge. So step lively now."

They passed through several more work areas. Not one of the workers glanced up or noticed the astonishing creature in Gwendolyn's charge. She took the blue gentleman to the commissary, where the workers on meal shift were taking a break. No sign of Slaggingham.

"Come along, Lovey-horns," she said. Without question, Auberon followed her to Slaggingham's office. She gave a sharp rap on the door, then let herself in.

Slaggingham sat in his ratty office, staring at some kind of viewing machine.

"That's it, Daniel, my boy," Slaggingham murmured at the image on the screen. "You show that blighter Timothy Hunter what's what."

"Reverend Slaggingham. I've brought you a gent." Gwendolyn eyed Auberon. "And if he's as strong as he is strange, you'll get a dozen men's work out of him."

"I'm pleased as carbolic punch to hear that," Slaggingham said. He may have been speaking to Gwendolyn, but his eyes stayed glued to the screen. "Stow his soul in the strong room and set his privileged carcass to work on the Extractor."

"Perhaps you'd like to look him over first,

Reverend? He's quite extraordinary, really. He's a king. And he's blue."

Slaggingham brought his hand down hard on the table with a clang. "Sister, please. I don't care if the waster has a brass monkey's tail. I'll inspect him later. I'm busy, do you hear? Busy! You have your instructions, dolly mop. Follow them."

"As you please, Reverend."

She spun around on her heels and left the room. Just outside the office door she stopped. She took in several short breaths in irritation. She slapped her forehead. "I can't believe I forgot."

She popped her head back inside the doorway. "Come with me, Lovey-horns," she ordered impatiently. If she hadn't given him the command, he would have stood in Slaggingham's office for hours. Auberon nodded and lumbered back into the tunnel after her.

Gwendolyn's annoyance made her walk quickly. "So I'm a dolly mop now, am I? Hmph. I may flash a smile and an ankle now and then, lordship. But I do it for the cause. I'm as respectable a seamstress as ever starved in a garret, I'll have you know."

They soon arrived at the locked globe storage room. Gwendolyn held out her hand. "Give me the globe, Lovey-horns." Auberon complied without question. Gwendolyn pulled a heavy iron key from her skirt pocket and unlocked the door.

"Stay here," she commanded. She slipped into the storage room. All that was inside were floor-to-ceiling shelves filled with globes just like the one she held in her hand. She carefully placed it among all the others, and studied it for a moment. *Maybe not* just *like the others*, she mused.

There was something different about his globe; something that made it stand out. She stepped closer and peered at it, noticing the sparkles and the light that glowed within. It seemed to hold something uncanny. Could it be . . . magical? She shook her head, trying to dispel the unsettling thoughts that arose unbidden as she contemplated the strange new addition to the collection, then stepped back out into the tunnel.

"You know what I remember clearest about my old life?" she told Auberon as she locked the door. She knew he wouldn't understand, but with the mood that she was in, she had the need to talk. "Not the work, though God knows I was hard at it from the day I was old enough to thread a needle." She led Auberon through the twists and turns of the tunnels, past work stations, past machines, past lives.

"It's the food I remember," she said. "With my mother and my sister and me all stitching away we could eat twice a day, most days. Cold boiled potatoes for breakfast. Hot boiled potatoes for supper. Not because we fancied them, but because they were cheap." She laughed bitterly. "And we were among the lucky ones." She shook her head. "You know what I want out of this queer little revolution, lordship? A world where no one has to choke down bloody boiled potatoes to keep body and soul together. That's my idea of paradise, Lovey-horns. Amusing, don't you think?"

Gwendolyn set him up at a work station, giving him precise instructions. When she was certain he understood his simple task, she turned to leave. Reaching the archway, she glanced back to make sure he was following her directions. He was. Looking at his elegant form, his velvet breeches and cloak, his soft hands, his silken hair, his gold jewels, a smirk crossed her face. "Just think," she called to him as she headed for the exit archway. "Here is your chance to see how the other half—" She cut herself off and shook her head. "No," she corrected herself. "How the other two thirds . . ." She stopped once again. "How the other ninety percent lives. That's what I call education."

*Aboveground London*

*Astonishing*, Tim thought. Underneath all that grime, soot, and dirt lurked the glowering boy he'd met in Free Country, Daniel. He was the one who had kept bugging him about Marya. And right now he sounded positively homicidal.

Tim coughed, feeling the dark particles clogging his throat, scratching inside his nose, his eyes. Tim tried not to breathe in, and protected his face with his arm. It didn't do much good.

"Tim, pull your shirt up and cover your mouth with it," Molly instructed. He could see she was shouting through her sweater.

Tim did as he was told, and the burning eased in his throat. His glasses served as some protection for his eyes.

*How can Daniel be producing all that soot? It's not as if he has a soot-making machine stowed somewhere.*

"All right, Hunter," Daniel shouted. "Now you're done for."

*Great*, Tim thought. *Just what I want to hear.*

Marya took a step toward the swirling mass that seemed to emanate from the angry boy.

"Daniel?" she called. "Is that really you?"

"Marya knows him?" Molly asked Tim.

"They're from the same place," Tim explained. "This is good. She might be able to help calm him down."

"What's happened, Daniel?" Marya asked. "Has someone been making you climb down chimneys again? You're all sooty."

"I was clean as a whistle when you done run off and left me."

"I didn't leave *you*, Daniel," Marya explained reasonably. "I left Free Country."

"Sure you did," Daniel snarled. "So you could cozy up to this double-crossing Hunter mongrel."

*Uh-oh*, Tim thought. *Instead of helping, talking to Marya might make Daniel even angrier.*

"Tim had nothing to do with it," Marya said. "I decided that I'd been a child long enough. That's all."

"Then how come I seen you chasing him not fifteen minutes ago. I saw it. Don't you deny it."

Tim was impressed with how calm and patient Marya was with Daniel.

"We were chasing him because he was running away," Marya replied. "He got all embarrassed when he found out I knew he was Molly's boyfriend."

*That really does sound lame*, Tim admitted to himself. *I have to quit that running-away thing once and for all. If Daniel doesn't succeed in doing me in, of course.*

Molly elbowed him in the side, then nodded toward Daniel. Tim realized what she was pointing out—Daniel had moved away from the unicorn.

Tim and Molly crept over to the stricken animal. Maybe they could clear its air passages and it would be okay. Tim kept an ear on the conversation between Daniel and Marya, hoping Marya would succeed in calming the boy down. Molly pulled tissues out of her jacket pocket and wiped the unicorn's eyes.

"It was my own fault, really," Marya said. "I should never have said anything. Molly told me he was funny about stuff like that."

Tim watched Daniel's face. *I wouldn't believe it if I was him*, Tim thought. *And if I did believe it, I'd think this Tim Hunter was one foolish moron. Running away isn't just pointless*, Tim realized. *It's dangerous in the long run.*

"You're lying, Marya," Daniel hissed. "'Cause you're afraid of me. 'Cause I'm strong now."

The unicorn snorted, which caught Daniel's attention. He glanced over to Molly and Tim. Waving his broom in fury, he stumbled backward away from Marya. "So that's the dodge, eh, Marya!" he shouted. "Soften me up while your Timothy undoes all my work!" He strode toward Molly and Tim.

Tim stood quickly. "Look out, Molly. Deranged chimney sweep heading our way."

"I see him." Molly stroked the unicorn's head.

It was a lot cleaner now. With Molly's coaxing, the creature scrambled to its feet. Only then did Molly stand up, too.

"Hey! You with the black hair," Daniel yelled. "Hook it or you'll catch some of what your pal's got coming."

"*Boy*friend," Molly corrected. "As of today, he is my boyfriend. Make a note. And here's another note. I used to have a unicorn. A toy one. It was plastic with a stupid rainbow mane."

"So?" Daniel sneered through his soot. He took a step closer, obviously trying to intimidate her. He was about six inches taller than Molly, but that didn't seem to faze her at all.

Tim hid a smile. *They must not have anyone like Molly O'Reilly where Daniel's from or he'd know better than to talk to her like that.*

"My big brother stole that unicorn," Molly continued. "Then he poured petrol on it and burned it to a crisp. Just for a lark."

"Hah! Did he now?" Daniel was positively smirking. He got right in her face. "Left you a-crying your little eyes out, did he?"

Molly didn't even flinch. "Yeah, I cried a little."

*Uh-oh, here it comes*, Tim thought. He actually felt sorry for Daniel.

"You should have heard *him*, though," Molly said. "After *I* got through with him." Molly gave

Daniel a hard, swift kick right where it hurt most.
Daniel let out a grunt and doubled over, then collapsed onto his knees.

Molly turned and walked back to Tim and the
unicorn.

"Awesome, Molly," Tim said.

Molly held her foot out to show Tim. "Yeah,
these boots are good for that sort of thing."

She stroked the wheezing unicorn's trembling
flanks. It was still struggling to breathe. "Let's
get this poor thing out of here."

Marya gazed sadly at Daniel, then moved
over to join them. "Is it okay?" she asked, patting
the unicorn's velvety nose.

"It will be," Tim promised her.

"Do you know a safe place to take the unicorn?" Molly asked Marya.

"Yes."

"Climb on."

Marya stared at her. "But I've never ridden a
horse."

"It's easy," Molly assured her. "Hold on with
your knees. Tightly, but not *too* tightly. You can
steer him by the mane, if you have to. But you
probably won't, since he's magic."

Tim and Molly boosted Marya onto the unicorn's back. She craned her neck to gaze back at
Daniel, who was now curled up on the pavement.

"What about Daniel?" she asked. "I want him to be okay, too." She shuddered. "He's so different now," she whispered. "So much angrier."

"Tim will sort him out," Molly said. "I hear he's magic, too."

She gave Tim a grin. Tim grinned back. It was so great to have his big secret out in the open. Molly was totally dealing with it. She was the best.

"Just get someplace safe," Molly told Marya.

"But—" Marya began to protest.

Molly slapped the unicorn's flank to get it going. It trotted away, its hooves clattering on the uneven pavement.

Tim watched them go, the unicorn disappearing around the corner. "Molly, shouldn't you be the one riding him? I mean, you're the one who grew up in the country."

"Uh, we didn't have unicorns on our farm, Tim," Molly replied, "just horses."

"You shouldn't have done that, missy," Daniel snarled.

Tim and Molly whirled around. Daniel was just a few feet away, the soot cloud even denser now. Tim could see tiny flames licking at the boy's clothes, but that didn't seem to bother Daniel at all.

He shook his filthy broom at them. "I ain't the

sort of cove people can kick around. Not anymore."

"Well, we're not the sort of people who appreciate being done over," Tim snapped.

"Done for," Molly corrected.

"Oh, right," Tim muttered. "Thanks." He raised his voice again. "We're not the sort of people who appreciate being 'done for.'"

"You watch your mouth, knave," Daniel snapped.

"Marya told you the truth," Tim said. "I haven't seen her since she hopscotched me to Free Country. In fact, I had no idea she was in London at all, until today. And besides, Marya isn't my girlfriend. Molly is."

*That wasn't so hard to say*, Tim realized. It just took a minute to get used to it. In fact, he definitely liked it.

Daniel's eyes narrowed. "You lie. Like a dog."

"You don't think I could be Tim's girlfriend?" Molly demanded. She looked ready to kick him again.

Tim threw up his hands in exasperation. "Why would I lie?"

"Because you're scared of me, that's why."

Tim laughed. He couldn't help it. "I'm not afraid of you," he said. The minute the words were out of his mouth he knew they were true, even though it would probably anger Daniel even more. "You know why? Because you are the first person I've met in a very long time who is even more confused than me."

"I ain't confused about nothing!" Daniel howled. He held up his broom and twirled. Soot began spewing out again, huge clouds of it. "And you're cat's meat!"

Daniel spun around and around. The wind whipped the soot into a massive cloud, darkening the sky, blackening the entire alley. Faster and faster Daniel twirled, and flames flickered out of him, as if he himself were on fire. Smoke poured out of him; his long hair, tendrils of flame; his ragged clothing invisible under the ash, soot, and fire. And it was all directed at Tim and Molly.

Tim desperately tried to battle the onslaught. *Concentrate*, he told himself. *Keep a clear passage to protect yourself. To protect Molly*. The smoke and soot cloud was so thick Tim couldn't see anything, not even Molly beside him. But he was still able to breathe.

He remembered when he had kept snow from falling on Kenny. That kind of magic was what was called for here—to create a protective bubble that would keep him and Molly safe and able to breathe.

He shut his eyes—not just to keep out the

burning soot and flames but to help him stay focused. He sent out his senses to feel Molly's presence; he needed to know how much area he needed to affect. *A barrier*, he thought. *That's what we need*. Something to block out this dirt, smoke, and soot that was flying everywhere. He envisioned the air itself fighting back, joining him to push the hot and scalding ash away.

He could hear Molly taking deep breaths beside him, and knew that he had done it. They were safe inside a pocket of clean air.

"I done it!" Daniel cheered. "No more Tim Hunter!" He slowed his whirling dance and lowered his broom. "That Slaggingham is a genius! Every word he said was true. Slaggingham and his machine made me a regular wonder!"

The soot settled over the street as Daniel calmed down. Tim and Molly stood side by side, sooty and sweaty from the heat of the attack but still breathing.

"Slaggingham?" Tim coughed. "Who's Slaggingham?"

Daniel gasped. "You—you ain't even singed." His body slumped. "It ain't fair." Daniel sank to the ground. "All right, beat on me, kick me again. I don't care."

"Uh, Daniel," Tim ventured. "We aren't going to hurt you. We just want you to calm down. You know, just be a bit less homicidal."

"I ain't no good," Daniel moaned. "Even this way I ain't no good at nothing."

Tim knelt down beside the miserable boy. "So you weren't always this sooty and furious?"

Daniel shook his head and wiped his nose on his sleeve. "Marya barely knew me," he said in sad confusion.

"She did say that you had changed," Molly said.

"What happened to you?" Tim asked.

Daniel shrugged wearily. "All I know is that I've felt sort of inside out since Slaggingham ran me through that Persona machine."

"The what?" Tim asked.

"Some invention he was harping on about. When I talked to him, down in his sewer. Said it would make me . . . better. But all I feel is different."

"Tim, take off your glasses," Molly said.

"My glasses?" Tim couldn't imagine what Molly had in mind. She knew he was practically blind without them.

"Yes," she insisted.

"Ooooh-kay." Tim reluctantly handed his glasses to her.

"Here." She held out the glasses to Daniel. "You may have to fiddle them around to do it, but take a look at yourself in their reflection."

Daniel took the glasses from Molly and turned them first one way then another. He gasped. "Th-that's me?" He dropped the glasses.

"Hey! Be careful with those." Tim bent down to retrieve his glasses, and Daniel gripped his arm so hard that Tim winced.

"You does magic!" Daniel blurted. "You can change me back! I can't go near Marya like this, not even to tell her I'm sorry. Please, you have to help me. You just have to."

The kneeling boy's pain was so raw, his need so transparent and overwhelming that Tim could not say no. Instead he said, "I'll try."

Tim stood over Daniel and studied him. *What's the best way to try to fix things for the guy?* Tim wondered. *Get rid of all that stinky soot for starters. Which means I have to figure out what it is.*

Tim held his hands out toward Daniel, taking care not to touch him. Gazing deeply into Daniel's sorrowful eyes, Tim let his mind open.

*Reach. Touch. Choking cinders and clinging soot. The acrid stickiness of tar beneath. These poisons do not coat the rags that clothe Daniel, they permeate them. Reach closer. Touch deeper. Brush aside the tatters. Sift through the crusting ash and sink into the stain. Find its source. Find its source. Learn its limits.*

A searing pain shot through Tim, causing him to cry out. Images flashed through his mind. The master's stick. The master's belt. The master's fist. Blow after blow felled him, for tiny mistakes, sometimes for no reason at all. Beatings when there was work to be done and when there wasn't. Wisps of straw set burning at the soles of his bare feet to drive him to climb the chimney faster. Salt water rubbed into his scraped raw knees and elbows to toughen them for the work. His only freedom the freedom to choose how his nights were spent. Locked in a closet in the orphanage with a cup of cabbage soup or hounded through dark streets as he scavenged for more nourishing fare.

It was suddenly clear to Tim: The cinders that spilled from Daniel were the remains of exhausted hope. The black soot he shed was the remnants of suffering Daniel could neither forget nor forgive. The fire was sullen rage, the deadly smoke, fear.

Tim wobbled on his feet, then took a step back, releasing the connection he had made so deeply with Daniel. He felt Molly's hand on his arm, and it brought him back to himself.

He blinked a few times, not wanting either of them to see how shaken he'd been by the glimpse into Daniel's life. And that the news he had to tell them wasn't good.

"So can you do it?" Daniel asked eagerly. "Can you set me back the way I was? Get rid of all this black muck?"

"Daniel," Tim said, "I really hate to be the one to say this, but that stuff that's on you—it's your soul. I don't think I can get it off you without . . . well, without killing you."

Daniel sank back onto his heels and covered his face with his hands.

"Is there anything you can do?" Molly asked, concern and sympathy on her face. Tim liked that she went from kicking Daniel to wanting to help him.

Tim sighed. "I can't say I'm looking forward to it, but yes, I do have an idea." He faced Daniel again. "There's one thing we can try. We've got to get this Slaggingham to run you through his machine again. In reverse, or something."

Daniel shuddered. "You won't catch me climbing into that glass coffin again. No thank you. I been through enough today." He tugged hard on the brim of his battered hat and pulled it low over his face. Tim could see the boy's lips sticking out in a pout.

"A pity party," Molly scoffed. "What fun."

"Isn't it, though," Tim said. Here he was trying to help, and the helpee wasn't helping at all.

Tim crouched down beside Daniel and lifted the hat brim. "I want to see this Slaggingham in person," he told Daniel. "And I'm not going to splash around the sewers all day to find him. You are going to take me to him. Now."

"Have you gone barmy?" Daniel scoffed. "He'll murder you, he will."

"Maybe, maybe not," Tim replied. "Can you zap us there, or should we be looking for a grate to crawl down?"

"Oh, I can take you straight to him. If that's what you really wants."

"It's what I wants—er, *want*." Tim stood back up and faced Molly. "If we're not back in an hour or so, you can start the ice cream expedition without us. Take Marya, if you can find her. I'm not sure if unicorns eat ice cream, though."

"Are you nuts?" Molly glared at Tim. "You can't go down there." She pointed at Daniel. "You heard what he said—this Slaggingham wants you dead. And you're just going to walk right into his lair?"

"I wouldn't call it a lair. It's more a factory, like," Daniel corrected.

Molly lifted her foot as a warning, and Daniel held up his hands in a placating gesture. Tim took her by the elbow and walked her a few steps away from Daniel.

"Molly, I'm certain the only way I can help Daniel is by running him back through that machine." He lowered his voice. "Besides, I don't think any of us are safe with him as he is. It's better if I nip this in the bud now."

As the words came out of his mouth he realized he was finally facing up to something in the moment. Instead of following his usual pattern of running away, he was dealing with the crisis dead-on.

Molly crossed her arms over her chest. "Then I'm coming with you."

"Oh, bad plan," Tim said. There was no way Tim would bring Molly along on this excursion underground. The fact that they were going after some bloke who invented machines that could do what had been done to Daniel meant they weren't dealing with anyone ordinary. He didn't want Molly anywhere near that.

But he knew her all too well—she wasn't one to sit back and let someone else go to the action. How could he convince her to stay behind?

"Look, I need you up here as backup," he explained. "If I don't come back after an hour, then come down and find me. If we're down there together now, there's no one to help later."

Molly narrowed her eyes as if she were trying to decide whether he was scamming her or serious.

"Okay," she said dubiously. "One hour only. And then I'm coming down after you."

"Thanks, Molly. Okay, Danny boy," Tim said, turning around. "Lead on." Silently he added, *I really hope I don't regret this.*

# Chapter Nine

*Underneath London*

REVEREND SLAGGINGHAM HAD BEEN tickled to see the transformation in his protégé, Daniel. He watched gleefully as the boy shouted out in rage at that blight on humanity, Timothy Hunter. Soot and cinders swirled everywhere—no one could survive that kind of attack. Now that he'd become an altered creature, perhaps Daniel would be able to withstand all that flame and ash. If not, more's the pity, but such is life.

A clanging alarm drew Slaggingham's attention away from his viewing machine. He glanced down at his watch. "Fume and choke me! I'm late! I should have inspected the Extractor three and a half minutes ago. How could I have missed it?"

Slaggingham pressed the button that caused

the panel to slide down, concealing the viewing machine again. Then, he hurried along to the main part of the underground factory. He went to inspect the bottling plant, admiring the perfectly symmetrical lines of the empty bottles on the conveyor belt. Snatching one up, he read the label aloud. "Slaggingham's Own Elixir of Happiness. Distilled and bottled in subterranean London."

He proudly scanned the area, pleased with the smooth production, the clockwork organization. All was in order.

He noticed a worker he didn't recognize at the controls. Slaggingham had never seen the likes of this guy before. The fellow was over seven feet tall, blue, and had ram's horns on his head. And the clothing he wore—it was like those of the troubadours in books: velvet doublet, slippers, long cloak. Who could he be?

"How did you get in here?" he demanded. A genius such as the reverend always had to be on the lookout for spies and saboteurs.

"The woman brought me," the worker replied in a flat tone, without stopping his work.

"Oh, and what woman might that be?"

"She who trapped my soul in a globe of crystal," the blue gentleman replied.

Of course, Slaggingham remembered—hadn't Gwendolyn mentioned bringing in an unusual specimen? She was certainly right about that.

"Gild my lily, but you'd pack them in at the circus. Who were you? And why would the likes of you choose to go slumming in London town?" Slaggingham peered at the creature, having a new and terrible thought. "Are you one of the Hunter brat's creatures?" he rasped.

"I was Auberon, High King of Faerie. I fled my realm to escape a longing more insistent than my soul could bear. I was no one's creature until your servant took my soul."

"So you were a king, eh?" Slaggingham stroked his stubbly chin. "I can't say I ever had the pleasure of enslaving an actual monarch before. Happy, were you?"

"If my soul had known happiness in Faerie, do you suppose it would have driven me here?"

"But you must have been happy, you infernal lumpet," Slaggingham snapped. "You were a bloody king! Lived in a palace, I reckon."

"Yes."

"Had your scurvy breakfast served up on a silver tray."

"Yes."

"But you weren't happy."

"No."

"My, what a sad story. Snap my grommets, if it hasn't got me feeling something close to sorry for you." Slaggingham shook his head. "Well, Brother Hornhead, since your previous life was such a prime sink of misery I offer you this: When my merchandise has spoiled the lives of a few more surface dwellers, and my Extractor soaks up enough of their lost happiness to commence distillation and bottling, I'll give you your own pint of happiness to wash the gloom from your guts. What do you say to that, Brother Hornhead?"

"When will you give me back my soul?"

Slaggingham waggled a finger at Auberon. "Tut-tut. Now that would be telling, wouldn't it? Ah, I best be getting back to my rounds."

Slaggingham continued on. There were so many machines to inspect! He strolled along a catwalk to the controls of one of the machines. He held his lantern up to read the dials.

"This reading can't be right," he sputtered. "The extractive terminals have been operational now for months. And the surface dwellers have never been so miserable, so we should be swilling in gallons of spare happiness by now. I should be swimming in the stuff."

He paced the catwalk trying to piece together why the machine was not functioning as it should. "Perhaps I've made the reservoir's sensor float too heavy," he muttered. He felt his artificial heart beating triple time, which he knew was not good for it, might spring a sprocket or two. Self-doubt, the most diabolical sort of emotion, threatened him at every turn. Whenever he suspected he had gone awry in his thinking, worried that perhaps he was not the genius he had always imagined himself to be, he forced the troublesome thoughts aside as best he could. Such ideas were deadly dangerous.

He concentrated on the problem at hand and peered into the bowels of the crotchety machine. "Ah! That's the answer. I knew I was taking a chance using balsa wood."

A metallic clinking behind him caught Slaggingham's attention. He turned to see screws fling themselves out of their spots, and then a grate popped open. A metal hand with screwdrivers and pliers for fingers appeared, and Awn the Blink, Slaggingham's nemesis—troublemaker extraordinaire—pulled himself out of the tiny space.

"Balsa wood, was it?" Awn the Blink asked. "I thought it tasted a bit organic."

"You!" Slaggingham growled.

"That's right, sir. Awn the Blink, in person. And not precisely at your service."

"You've gone too far," Slaggingham fumed. "Seventy-seven ratcheting years it took me to build this Extractor! I won't have my beauty tampered with by an antennae-topped figment of

Timothy Hunter's imagination."

"So you figured out it was I who'd done it, eh?" Awn the Blink said. "You're smarter than you look. And 'cause I'm a kindly soul, I'll help you out. I can tell you what's wrong with your invention."

"Crank me! Would you?"

"I will indeed."

Slaggingham beamed. "You know the moment I clapped eyes on you, Mr. Blink, I said to myself, now there's an honest son of toil. Why, look at the hands on him. Those stalwart hands aren't stained with the blood of the oppressed laboring classes, by jingo, those hands—"

Awn the Blink cut him off. "Fifty pounds, squire. That's the deal. Take it or leave it."

Slaggingham's jaw dropped open. Then he snapped it shut with a bang and his eyes narrowed. "Forty pounds, and not a farthing more."

"Sixty," Awn the Blink countered.

"Very well, you profiteer. Fifty it is."

"Seventy-five."

"Tinker and blast." Slaggingham threw up his hands in defeat. "Done!" Slaggingham pulled a wallet from inside his jacket pocket. Muttering oaths under his breath, he counted out the bills into Awn the Blink's metal palm. "Pirate. Thief."

Awn the Blink ignored the name-calling, and double-checked the number of bills. Satisfied, he shoved them into the back pocket of his baggy, grease-stained blue jeans.

Slaggingham tapped his foot impatiently. "Well?" he snapped.

Awn the Blink grinned. "All right, guv'nor, now that we've taken care of the business portion of our conversation. About this Anti-Tantalic Extractor apparatus of yours."

"Yes?" Slaggingham hated the eagerness in his voice, knowing it revealed the fear behind the question. Confound it! He shouldn't need explanations from the likes of Awn the Blink! His own scheming blueprint of a brain should be capable of solving every conundrum.

"The design is a pippin," Awn the Blink declared, "and the construction is every bit a wonder."

Slaggingham beamed. "Of course, of course. No need for compliments." His chest puffed out a bit. Perhaps he'd misjudged the tool-fingered contraption.

"Your problem is entirely conceptual."

This caught Slaggingham up short. "Oh?" His eyebrows rose. A conceptual problem? Impossible! That would mean the problem had been there all along and he had never seen it. In fact, one might hazard to say that if it were a "conceptual problem," then it was he himself who had caused it. If that were the case, how could he live with himself?

Awn the Blink patted the Extractor, his metal fingers clanking on the machine. "This setup you got would work fine for extracting particles or gases from the atmosphere. But happiness? Hah!"

"Wh-what do you mean?" Could the little blighter be right? Was there a flaw in the concept itself? *What could I have missed?* Slaggingham wondered.

"Emotions don't float about in the air like flipping molecules, squire. You were doomed to failure from the start."

"B-b-but—" Slaggingham sputtered. Error was just not possible! Not possible!

Awn the Blink continued without even a pause. "And even if you could catch and bottle the stuff, what good would that do *you*?" He pointed a screwdriver-tipped finger at Slaggingham. "You've turned yourself into a mechanism with these whatsits of yours. Sure, it allowed you a longer life than required by most, but at the end of the day, where did it get you?"

Now Slaggingham simply gaped openmouthed at Awn the Blink.

"You couldn't use the elixir even if it could exist. You're not built to swallow, much less digest."

"Tippy-tappy torque wrench!" Slaggingham moaned, understanding hitting him all at once. He clapped a hand to his forehead. "What a fool I've made of myself."

It was true—he was a complete and utter failure. He had worked for all these years—decades, nay, a *century*!—on a stinking design flaw. And even if he had managed to wrest happiness from the very air, the transformations he had wrought on himself in his efforts to achieve his goals had made him a freak, who could never benefit from his hard work. The irony of his predicament pained him to his very bloodless core.

He unbuttoned his vest, flicked the bolts on his metal chest, and yanked out his heart. He stared at the thing—the cold mechanical thing. It clicked methodically in his hand, tiny lights pulsing. Slaggingham yanked on the chain that ran though his body instead of veins, so that he could bring the heart up to his face.

"Oh, even the most cunningly engineered plans, they will go astray, curse them!" His grip on the heart tightened; springs popped out of place.

"Curse them," he bellowed, throwing back his head and letting out a howl. He snapped the heavy chain right out of his body and flung the mechanical heart to the floor. He glared down at it. "You foul thing, you have betrayed me." He stomped it hard, mechanical pieces scattering all around.

"Curse them!" he whispered as he collapsed into the corner. Awn the Blink grinned, then hopped back into the grate.

Tim peered anxiously down into the muck. The sewers were dark and they stank, and he really didn't want to think about what might be under that water. He wanted to get this business with Daniel over with, go back above ground, and take about thirty showers.

Water dripped from the damp, vaulted ceilings overhead, making plop-plop-plopping noises. *Isn't dripping water some sort of torture?* Tim was beginning to understand why: The repetitive sound was really irritating. The whole place gave Tim the creeps.

Daniel must have noticed Tim's dubious expression. "This is just the entrance into the underground system," he explained. "Wait until you see the factory and the machines and thingies."

They moved farther along the tunnel, and Tim saw that it branched in several directions. *How big is this place?* he wondered.

"This way." Daniel bounded through an archway, and Tim followed. Daniel obviously knew his way around—he even managed to avoid tripping over uneven patches and the messiest of the muck.

Once through the archway Tim discovered that he and Daniel stood on a long catwalk running the length of an enormous, vaulted room. At the center was a large pile of junk—pieces of twisted metal and gadgets clumped together like some kind of weird sculpture. The place was deserted, and the few lights flickered as if they were running out of electricity.

"I thought you said this was a factory," Tim said.

"It was." Daniel sounded uncertain. "Mine and Slaggingham's. We were partners."

"I don't know, Daniel. It doesn't look like your factory is making much of anything at the moment."

"Yes, I grant you that."

"Was that the machine Slaggingham put you through?" Tim asked, nodding toward the massive pile of metal. He hoped not, since it looked like it needed extensive repair, and he was pretty sure the manual would be nowhere around.

"No, it was farther in," Daniel explained. He led Tim along the catwalk and through another archway. Now they climbed down a metal ladder, and found more tunnels.

*It's a regular city down here*, Tim observed. He supposed it could have once been a factory; there was certainly enough stuff around and space. But it sure didn't look like it was still open for business.

Daniel seemed as confused as Tim. "It's never been so quiet in here," he confessed. "Before, there was all this whirring and banging and—" He held up a hand. "Wait . . . hear that?"

Tim strained his ears to listen. Daniel was right—it was faint, but it was there. A small *fzzzt, fzzzt*, sizzling sound.

"This way." Daniel dashed forward in the dark tunnel, then came to such a sudden stop that Tim banged into him.

"What is it?" Tim asked. Then he saw the heap in the corner. He had thought it was just a pile of rags and more metal scrap, but it wasn't. It was—

"Slaggingham." Daniel gasped. "He ain't all there."

"No, I guess you could say that."

Someone—some*thing*—lay sprawled in the corner. This Slaggingham must have once had a face, Tim noted, but whatever the creature had used for skin had peeled off in large chunks, revealing silvery metal underneath. Its chest was sprung open, so Tim could see the inner workings. *It must be some kind of robot*, Tim realized. *Or some combination of cyborg and human*. Bolts, sockets, and nuts crunched under their feet as Daniel and Tim moved closer.

"Daniel, is that you?" the creature rasped. "You're right as rain. I'm not all here. Look at me, boy, I'm brokenhearted. Short-circuited."

The sizzling sound that they had heard came from the electrical units shorting out Slaggingham's inner workings. Tim was afraid if they got too close they'd get singed by the random sparks shooting out of its head and chest.

"Let this be a lesson to you, lad," Slaggingham wheezed. "Never trust a machine. Or try to be one."

"I won't, sir," Daniel replied, sounding choked up.

"Still, you put that Hunter brat down like the dog he is just for me, didn't you, lad? Sent him off to meet his maker in a perishing fountain of sparks, eh? That's my boy. You done good, lad. You make me proud."

Tim glanced at Daniel and saw tears in the boy's eyes. Daniel cleared his throat. "You bet I did, Reverend." He looked at Tim, a weak, sad smile on his face. "He won't be bothering you no more, and that's the gospel truth."

Tim backed up into the shadows so that there was no chance that Reverend Slaggingham would spot him. He knew that Daniel needed this man to be proud of him—to think that Daniel had accomplished the task he'd been asked to do. It was a harmless lie, one to make an old—well, not *man*, exactly, but *father figure*—happy before he expired. *What's the harm in that?*

A groaning, screeching sound filled the air, followed by a deep rumbling.

"Blimey, what's that?" Daniel asked.

"That would be the river ripping back through the tunnels," Slaggingham creaked. "You see, the infernal flood-control system is dysfunctional, since—since . . ."

With a droning, whirring sound, each of the pulsing lights in Slaggingham blinked off. A few sparks shot out, then silence.

"He's gone," Daniel murmured.

Tim gave Daniel a moment. When he saw the sooty chimney sweep wipe his eyes, Tim laid a hand on his shoulder. "I guess we'd better get out of here. That water sounds like it's getting pretty close."

"Aye." Daniel whirled to face Tim again. His jaw was set and there was a strange glint in his eyes. "I'm going to hotfoot it out of here, just in front of the flood. But you, you girl-stealing slacker, you can just stay down here and drown. You may have had me fooled for a while there, but Slaggingham reminded me of what's what."

"But—"

"He's the only one who's ever believed in me, and I'll be danged if I'm going to let him down. So when you sees old Slaggingham in the next life, you tell him who fetched you there. Just like I promised."

Daniel raised his broom in front of Tim and twirled it. Soot and dust flew everywhere, blinding Tim and setting him coughing. When the dust cleared, Tim was alone in the tunnel.

# Chapter Ten

TIM SHOOK HIS HEAD. "This death wish of yours, Tim," he scolded himself. "You've really got to do something about it." The sound of the water grew closer. *And do something about it soon.*

Giving Slaggingham one last glance, Tim began to explore the tunnels. There were a few flickering lanterns still hanging from the walls, but most of the electric lights had burned out. Steep shadows blanketed everything, making it hard to tell where there were doors or new tunnels, or where any sort of exit might be.

"Why did you do it, Tim?" he asked himself. "If I've told you once, I've told you a thousand times: Never trust anyone who has at any point wished you dead. Especially juvenile delinquent chimney sweeps."

His voice echoed in the dark passageway. The only other sounds were the lapping water rising and his sloshing footsteps.

"Oh, calm down, Tim," he continued. "Things could be worse, you know. After all, it's not quite pitch-dark in here, and the water isn't up to the ceiling. Yet."

He came to an archway and peeked through. Another huge machine loomed in the center of the room. Spotting a metal ladder, he hurried around the machine and climbed up onto a catwalk. That should keep him above the water for a while.

"I'd be all set if I had a torch and a pair of swimming trunks. Oh, and someone who would kindly show me the way out of here." He came to a dead end. "Gosh, Tim. I don't know. That seems like a lot to ask for." He turned around and walked back the way he had come. *Hang on, something looks different here.* He felt along the wall and found a handle. He grinned. "Would you settle for a door?"

It was so dark he hadn't noticed the door the first time he passed it. He pushed hard against it, but it didn't budge.

"Yeah, I'd settle for a door if it weren't locked," he said. He kicked the door in frustration. *Unless* . . . he thought. He felt himself suddenly edgy with nervous energy. Should he or shouldn't he?

"Come on, this is really stupid," he admonished himself. "You shouldn't be afraid of trying to magic your way out of this. You did all right up there with Daniel."

He slumped against the damp wall. "Yeah, but you blew it big time with Molly and Marya—freezing them like that," he reminded himself. "You were just lucky you were able to undo whatever it was that you did." He shook his head irritably. "Listen to you, Tim, you're babbling. Are you going to drown here? Or are you going to take Molly out for ice cream?"

He knew he couldn't take too long. Molly was going to come after him in an hour. And she was always as good as her word. If she came down here looking for him now . . .

His heart thumped hard in his chest—fast and then faster as he thought of the danger his absence would put Molly in. He had to get out—if only to save Molly.

A grate suddenly popped open beside him, making him jump. A strange little guy with tools for hands, nails for hair, and a body composed of all kinds of sprockets and stray parts climbed out of the grate. The creature had goggles instead of eyes, but wore regular clothes: dirty jeans and a filthy T-shirt.

Tim stepped back. This *thing* looked like it could be related to old Slaggingham back there. Did this creature also want him dead?

"Master Tim!" The little guy grinned. "Why, hello! It's just me, Awn the Blink. I brought that torch you were hoping for. Couldn't arrange the swim trunks for you, though. Sorry." The guy handed Tim a big, reassuring flashlight.

"Thanks, Mr., uh, Blink. Mr. Awn." Tim clicked on the flashlight and instantly felt better. Now he could see his surroundings more clearly, although the sights didn't exactly fill him with joy. He peered over the side of the catwalk. The water was up to about six feet now.

"Don't mention it," Awn the Blink said. "It would have been pointless to scrap old Slaggingham if it was just to watch you drown, sir."

Tim swung around the flashlight so that it shone on Awn the Blink. "You scrapped Slaggingham?"

"Yes, indeedy. He was dead set on having you murdered, see. And I couldn't stand for that, naturally."

"Uh, naturally. *I* certainly wouldn't."

"So I put him out of commission. Took me a while to figure out how, but I did. I broke his heart, see. So then he broke his heart, too. First I did it conceptually, then he did it for real. If you follow me."

"I don't actually follow you, but I'll take your word for it. And thank you."

"Any time, any time. We can't have you dying on us, can we? After all, if you go, we all go."

"Mr. Blink? One question, if you don't mind."

"Certainly, lad. Wait one moment though—this will most likely drown you out."

Holding up one hand to stop Tim from speaking, Awn the Blink stuck one of his mechanical digits into the lock, twisted it, then pulled the door open.

"Wow." Tim whistled. "Good job."

"Thanks, my boy."

"Listen, do we know each other? I have the strangest feeling I've met you before. And you sort of seem to know me, too."

"Good one, Master Tim. I've noted the query, and the answer will be forthcoming ASAP. Namely, once you're out of danger. Should have upward of five minutes before the river really comes slashing through here."

"Ah, loads of time, then."

"Enough, Master Tim. Just enough, I'd say."

Tim followed Awn the Blink along the catwalk. Every now and then Tim peered over the railing. The water was rising faster now.

"You're quiet, Master Tim. Calculating revenge on that grubby little chimney weasel?"

"Nah. I feel sorry for the bloke," Tim replied. "I was really thinking how glad I am that I didn't have to swim in that muck. Thanks to you."

"No doubt. Be surprised if there weren't a ravenous boa constrictor or two down there."

"A boa constrictor? Down here?" Tim asked.

"Why, if I were a betting man, sir, I'd lay odds on it. Didn't you believe that there were boas down here when you were a sprout? Your old mate Jackie Frost had a baby one, remember? Kept it in the bathtub, till it had a go at his mum's cat one day. Then ker-flush! You and Jackie carried on something fierce once you found out. So Mrs. Frost told you that the sewers were a regular playground for boa constrictors and your old chum Squirmy, he'd be happy there. And you being a trusting lad, you believed the lady."

"Mr. Blink, are you trying to tell me that *everything* I used to believe in is real now? I mean, I've seen the Wobbly and the Narls, but—"

"And me, sir, don't forget me!"

"And *you* . . . That's why you seem so familiar! I remember you now!"

"Righto, I knew you would. You were three, maybe four, and your telly wasn't working. So you asked your dad, what's wrong with the telly. 'It's awn the blink' he says. And you, being an imaginative young sprout, you imagine me."

He gave a little bow. "An extraordinarily talented *un*-repairman. Coming and going as I please, disabling appliances with the greatest of ease."

He spun the tiny drills on the ends of his fingers, making a soft whirring sound. "And since the times I'm interfering with your telly seemed to be the only times your old dad paid attention to you, you figured I must be your friend. On your side, like. Which I am, young master, never doubt it."

"Gosh. Well, thanks." *So it's true*, Tim realized. *My imaginary friends have all come back to life, now that I've tapped into my magic.*

"Don't mention it," Awn the Blink said. "Besides, since you done me the favor of inventing me, I feel obliged to protect you, seeing as you are my creator and all. Kinda my life's work, as it were."

"Wow. Some people have guardian angels; I have Awn the Blink." Tim eyed the odd tool-configured fellow and grinned. "I think I got the best end of the deal!"

Awn the Blink smiled back. "Now, let's get you topside where you belong."

# Chapter Eleven

BROTHER SALAMANDER WAS ABOVE Gwendolyn on the ladder, grunting heavily as he shoved open the manhole cover. Gwendolyn squinted as the unaccustomed daylight broke into the darkness of the tunnels. Despite her trips to the surface, Gwendolyn was far more used to the environment underground. There were work lights below, of course, but the artificial illumination cast an eerie yellow-green glow, giving the factory workers the pallor of the sick and the dead. She could smell the change as the air from above ground made an effort to work its way down and as the contained atmosphere worked its way up.

Brother Salamander hoisted himself up and out onto the street. He peered back down at Gwendolyn. "Hand me up that lamp and my bag, girlie. And your basket. You'll need both hands to climb."

Gwendolyn did as she was told, then climbed up the ladder. Her skirt was soaked past the knees. She knew there was little time left before the river reclaimed its original territory below. She pulled herself out onto the sidewalk.

Brother Salamander squeezed water from his coveralls, and zipped open his soaking bag. "I hope they aren't all ruined," he muttered. He glanced at Gwendolyn, eyeing her basket. "What did you get out with? If you don't mind my asking."

"My pride."

The man snorted. "Wouldn't have thought that would have fit in a little basket like that."

Gwendolyn ignored his comment. It was none of his business that she'd brought her sewing tools with her. It was how she would keep her pride; she could go back to being an honest working girl like in the old days. "What have *you* got?" she asked him.

"I made out the best I could. There wasn't time to pick and choose."

"No, there wasn't."

He rummaged in his bag. "These should keep me in grog and victuals for a fortnight at least. What do you think, girlie?" He held up a crystal globe. "Shall I sell 'em as paperweights? Lucky charms? Gypsy fortune-telling balls?"

"Oh no!" Gwendolyn gasped. "The gents!"

Grabbing the lantern, Gwendolyn quickly clambered back through the hole leading underground.

"Hey! Hey! That's my carbide lamp, you minx!" Brother Salamander shouted after her. "Bring that back!"

"I will!" Gwendolyn hurried through the tunnels. She tripped on the hem of her soggy dress. "Confound these skirts. And these ridiculous shoes." She sat on the wet walk. "You can't climb in them and you can't run in them. And you certainly can't swim."

She opened her sewing basket. She grabbed a pair of scissors and cut the skirt of her dress to a shocking length above her knees. *Sometimes a girl had to forget modesty for practicality's sake*, she reasoned. She unbuttoned her heeled boots, and ripped the bottoms of her tights so that she wouldn't slip.

"Surely I can't have been the only one who remembered that the gents can't fend for themselves," she hoped out loud as she ran.

She raced to the main room of the factory, where hundreds of men normally worked as drones tending the machinery, stoking the fires, oiling the gears, flipping the switches, loading, unloading, starting, stopping, restarting. Over and over and over again.

She arrived at the catwalk, where Reverend Slaggingham usually observed his workers, and she gazed down. Her stomach clenched and she felt a sob rise in her chest.

"Drowned like rats," she murmured, looking at the floating bodies. The river had flooded into this area first, and the water had risen over twelve feet. The men weren't capable of thinking for themselves, not once their souls were removed. They could do only as they were instructed, and all they were instructed to do was work. So despite the rising water, none of them had left his station.

Gwendolyn buried her face in her hands. "And who swindled them out of their souls and their free will with a smile and a flash of stocking? Who was the little jezebel who—" She cut off her self-recriminations as she remembered there was a very special prisoner on one of the platforms down here.

He'd been different. Not because he was blue, but because he had tried to help her when that man had been so forward. Sure, he was like the rest of the spoiled and pampered aristocracy, but he'd extended himself to intervene on her behalf.

Could he still be alive? "Lovey-horns!" She raced along the catwalk through archway after archway. "Auberon! Auberon, can you hear me?"

She climbed down the metal stairs to where Auberon had been stationed. It was just barely underwater. There was still hope. She placed the lantern and her basket on a step and dove in.

She immediately spotted him. Maybe he'd only just gone under. Maybe she really could rescue him. She wrapped her arms around his chest and kicked hard. With a huge effort, she burst through the surface of the water. He was so big and his water-laden velvet clothing made him so heavy. He weighed her down, threatening to sink them both with his dead weight.

"Swim, lordship!" she ordered.

Without a soul, he was dazed, useless. But he didn't seem to be suffering from the lack of air, at least. "Swim?" he repeated.

She struggled to keep her head above water. "You may not need to breathe, but I do! Swim. That's your new order."

He took such a strong stroke that he pulled out of her grip. She quickly swam to the steps and climbed out of the deep pool. Auberon continued swimming around the space.

"Oh, gracious sakes, Lovey-horns," she said

with exasperation. "Come out of there." While Gwendolyn wrung some of the water from her skirts and pushed her long wet hair out of her face, Auberon swam to the steps and climbed up onto the catwalk. He stood silent and imposing in front of her.

"Well, aren't you going to thank me, your majesty?" Gwendolyn asked. "Or were you enjoying yourself down there?"

"I have not been instructed to thank you," Auberon replied, "or to enjoy myself. So I do neither."

"Oh, dear. This will never do." She studied the amazing creature. He was beautiful, in his own peculiar way, and even without a soul he still carried himself with dignity.

"There's no work for you here now, Loveyhorns," Gwendolyn explained. "So be a lamb and come along. You're going to help me find your soul. You probably have more use for it than anyone else is likely to."

Auberon nodded gravely, though Gwendolyn knew that all he comprehended in the state he was in was that she'd given him orders.

"Now, you'll probably have to swim for it, since the waters will have risen in that portion of the factory," Gwendolyn explained, leading him along the catwalk. "But since you managed being submerged far more efficiently than I, that should be right simple."

*No*, she thought, *finding his soul shouldn't be a problem*. The real problem would be in getting it back to where it belonged. That was a trick she had simply never learned. She'd never had a reason to before.

# Chapter Twelve

MARYA STROKED THE WHITE mane of the unicorn as they stood in the empty studio at the Swan Dance School. Tim had told her to go somewhere safe and this was the safest place she knew. Dancing made her feel whole and strong. That's how she would need to feel if she had to face Daniel again.

"Daniel is really very nice. I mean, he used to be," she told the unicorn. She wasn't sure if the repetitive action of combing the unicorn's mane with her fingers was more soothing to her or to the unicorn. She could tell, though, that it was comforting to them both. "But it makes my stomach hurt just knowing that he's out there." She felt terrible for saying such a thing, but it was the truth. "He's not bad, exactly. It's more that . . ." She thought for a moment, trying to find the exact words to make the unicorn understand. "Well, he

was always so needy. As if he couldn't like himself, so you had to like him *for* him."

She rested her forehead lightly against the
unicorn's flank. "I can't do that anymore. I have a
life, now. A real life. Not a Free Country life."

She lifted her head again and patted the unicorn. "You don't want to hear about this, do you?
You'd rather have an apple, I'll bet."

Kneeling down, she rummaged through her
bag for an apple. She held it out to the unicorn.
The unicorn sniffed the apple, then delicately took
it from Marya. It crunched down on the fruit,
eating it in two quick bites. Then it nuzzled
Marya's arm, tickling her.

Giggling, Marya asked, "Want another?" She
reached back into her bag, but this time her fingers
closed on a small statue. She pulled out the ballerina statue and gazed at it sadly. It was her good-
bye present from Daniel when she left Free Country.

"Oh, Daniel," she sighed. "I hate saying this,
but I really hope I've seen the last of you."

She suddenly noticed bits of ash and soot
drifting toward her, piling up around her feet. She
stood up quickly and whirled around.

Daniel loomed just inside the doorway of the
studio.

"How long have you been standing there?"
Marya asked.

"Long enough," he replied.

She took a step toward him. "Daniel," she said gently.

"Don't you act all sweet with me." He shook the sooty broom at her, sending her into a coughing fit. "Don't you dare! If you knew the half of it, Marya. I've made a fool of myself over you. A perishing fool!"

The unicorn's tail flicked, and its ears twitched. It snorted a few times. "I wish you wouldn't yell," Marya told Daniel. "It upsets the unicorn." She stroked its velvety nose, trying to calm it, trying to calm herself. She wondered how she would ever manage to calm Daniel.

"I ain't yelling," Daniel snapped. "You ain't never heard me yell. I never raised my voice to you. Never!"

"Okay, you're not yelling," Marya said, even though Daniel's voice was loud and made her nervous.

Daniel sidled past the unicorn. "You keep that ruddy animal in line," he muttered, shooting the unicorn a dirty look.

The dust cloud surrounding him made Marya's throat burn. She wondered how it must feel to be Daniel, so unhappy, with soot swirling around him and his soul all twisted.

"You ain't talking so much now that you have

to do it to my face, I see," Daniel sneered. "What's the matter? Run out of lies?"

"I've never lied," Marya said. "Not to you. Not to anyone. Except maybe to myself."

"When I think of how you used to smile at me, and talk to me. All to keep me hoping—"

"Daniel," Marya cut him off. "I smiled at you because I liked you. I talked to you because I wanted to. And I left because I had to."

"Know what the talk is back in Free Country?" Daniel snarled. "They said you cut and run because I kissed you. That you left to get far away from me. That's what they all say."

"That's crazy," Marya said. "You know that isn't true. I left because I didn't want to play for the rest of my life. That's the only reason."

"Play?"

"Play, play, play all the time. That's life in Free Country. I wanted to grow up, Daniel. I wouldn't go back for anything."

"Well, I would. If I could."

"What do you mean? Can't you go back? Daniel, that's terrible. What happened?"

"*You* happened!"

Marya shook her head in confusion. "I don't understand."

"Don't you?" He took a step closer. "I changed for you. I became this for you! This . . . *thing*!

They'll never let me back in like this. And for
what? What a fool I've been. All for you." He took
a step toward her. "Now, because of you, I can't
ever go back!"

He raised his hand as if he intended to slap
her. Marya threw up her hands to protect herself.
At the same moment, the unicorn whinnied and
reared up on its hind legs. It came back down
between Daniel and Marya. Lowering its head, it
touched Daniel at the heart with the tip of its
horn. Daniel shuddered as if an electric jolt had
shot through him.

"Oh no!" Marya cried. She didn't understand
what was happening to Daniel or how the unicorn
had moved so quickly. It all happened in a matter
of seconds. "Please don't hurt him," she whispered. The unicorn whickered softly.

Marya watched in amazement as Daniel's
eyes rolled upward, and he stood paralyzed in the
center of a golden haze. He seemed to be suspended in a cloud of glitter and sparkles. All the
soot evaporated, and the healthy glow returned to
his flesh.

The unicorn stamped the floor with a front
hoof and then stepped back. Daniel wobbled on
his feet, dazed.

He felt . . . different. Lighter. More like his old

self. Could that be possible? He gazed down at his jacket, his trousers. They were soggy from his tramp down in the tunnels, but they were no longer covered in soot. "Blimey!" he cried. "I've been cured. That magic horsie touched me and it made me better."

He looked at the unicorn, its glinting eyes solemn and mysterious. "Sorry I tried to singe you when last we met," he told the unicorn, hanging his head shamefully. "I—I wasn't myself then. I am truly grateful for what you done."

He glanced around the room. His heart hurt to see how Marya shrank away from him in the corner of the dance studio. She was clutching the long wooden barre that ran the length of the room, staring at him, her green eyes wide. He couldn't tell if she was frightened or not.

*Of course she's frightened, you fool!* he admonished himself. *You nearly hit her. Marya. Your angel. You almost struck her a blow. How can she stand to even be in the same room with you?*

"Marya," he said, his voice choking. "I—I'm so sorry. You know I never meant to—"

"But you did mean to," Marya said. "The unicorn stopped you."

Daniel's shoulders slumped. She was right. He was angry and he had raised his hand to her.

He wanted to believe that he would never have actually hit her, that he would have stopped himself. But he didn't know for certain. "You know I wasn't really me, just then," he said, his eyes still fixed on the floor.

"I know," Marya replied sadly. "But it's still not okay."

Daniel's heart clutched. He'd done it for sure, this time. There was no way that she would ever forgive him. How could she, when he couldn't forgive himself? He had to go away, stay away from her. Until he could be really, really good.

"Maybe . . . maybe you can go back to Free Country now," Marya suggested softly.

Daniel shrugged. He didn't trust himself to speak. He shuffled toward the door. As he opened it, he heard Marya say "Good-bye, Daniel."

Without turning around, without facing her, he said, "Good-bye," and walked out the door.

Marya watched him go. She knew he was sorry; she knew he was sad. She was sad, too, but that still didn't mean he could ever, ever hit her, or even try to. His anger was dangerous.

He had once been so kind, so sweet. Even in Free Country, though, she could sense his dark sadness pulling at him. Maybe now that he realized she couldn't be whatever it was he wanted her to be, he would finally be able to start a new life for himself.

She gazed around the soot-covered studio. The unicorn lay down in the corner, watching her. It seemed calm, relaxed even, now that Daniel had gone. Marya was still unsettled, though. Her feelings were jumbled inside her.

Rubbing her bare feet in the soot as if it were the rosin she used on her pointe shoes, she began to dance. She danced Daniel's pain, and her sorrow for him. She danced a sense of loss and good-byes. She danced gratitude to Tim and the unicorn, and for finding friends like Molly. She danced and danced and danced.

"Upsa-daisy, mind your elbows," Awn the Blink instructed Timothy. He helped Tim out of a manhole into the street.

"Air!" Tim cheered. "Sunlight!"

"Tim!" Molly charged toward them. "You're okay! I was just about to come down there after you!"

She skidded to a stop when she spotted Awn the Blink. "Er, hello," she said.

Tim grinned. "Molly, this is Awn the Blink. He just saved my life."

"Hello, miss," Awn the Blink greeted Molly.

"Uh, hi," Molly said, a smile spreading across her face. "Gee, Tim. I guess now that you're a magician you run in some wild circles."

"And not all of them human," Tim agreed.

"Thanks for saving Tim's life," Molly told Awn the Blink.

"Oh, Master Tim is exaggerating. He was just gearing up to magic his way out of the chimney weasel's trap when I turned up."

He pulled a grimy handkerchief from his pocket and wiped his goggles. "And now I'll take my leave of you. Lots of things to unrepair, you know." He winked and dropped back down underground, pulling the manhole cover over him.

The minute Awn the Blink vanished, Molly spun around and glared at Tim, her eyes flashing. "So it *was* a trap," she fumed. "Just as I suspected." She put her hands on her hips and shook her head. "I see he really appreciated all you tried to do for him."

"You know, this may sound weird," Tim said, "but I think he was just trying to be honest. And make an old man proud."

Molly snorted.

"Really." Tim scratched his head, puzzling it out. "He told Slaggingham he killed me. So it was kind of like honoring a dying man's request. And then, I think he felt bad about lying. So he had to make it come true. See?"

Molly crossed her arms over her chest and

rolled her eyes. "Well, I can't believe you were too selfish to let him kill you," she said, her voice dripping with sarcasm. "You ought to be ashamed of yourself."

She spun around on her heels and stomped away. "I don't suppose it ever occurred to you to feel sorry for the ice cream shopkeepers?" she called back to Tim. "They could go out of business before you ever get around to taking a person for her ice cream!"

"Molly, wait." Tim ran after her. "Please."

Molly stopped, but she still kept her back to him.

"All right, it was risky," Tim admitted.

"Hmph."

"Probably stupid," Tim added.

"I'll say. But also brave and kind, too," she added in a softer tone.

Tim smiled at her back.

Molly turned and waggled a scolding finger at him. "If Daniel had managed to kill you, I'd never have forgiven you! And I can't believe you kept this whole magic thing secret from me!"

Tim sighed. "I know. I kept trying to tell you, ever since I found out a few months ago. Really. You don't know how many times. But the words just wouldn't come out of my mouth."

Molly grinned, and Tim could tell everything

was okay between them. "Sounds like typical you," she said. "So now what do we do?"

"Let's go make sure Marya and the unicorn are okay," Tim said. "Daniel might have gone looking for her."

"You're right about that." Molly shivered. "That boy is way obsessed."

"You know Marya better than I do. Do you have any idea where she would take the unicorn?"

Molly thought for a moment, then her face brightened. "I know exactly."

Molly grabbed Tim's hand and together they raced along the streets, Molly leading the way. Tim took in deep breaths. *I never thought I'd actually think the air in East London could smell so great*, Tim thought.

They arrived at the Swan Dance Studio and discovered Marya peering out one window, the unicorn's head hanging out the other.

"Now that's a sight," Molly commented.

"Get used to it, if you plan to hang around me," Tim warned her. "You'll find yourself seeing all sorts of unusual things."

Moments later, Marya and the unicorn were down on the street with Tim and Molly. She explained what had happened with Daniel. "But at least he's back to being himself again," Marya said.

"And that's a good thing?" Molly muttered.

"I don't know about you, but I am ready for that ice cream," Tim said.

"What flavor do you think the unicorn will like?" Marya asked.

"Hay? Carrot?" Molly guessed. The three friends walked along the street laughing, followed by the unicorn.

Tim hadn't felt this good since he discovered he was magic. He wasn't hiding anything anymore, he was with friends, and his latest adventure had ended pretty well, all things considered.

They rounded a corner and Tim stopped. Two very unusual figures approached them. One was a sopping-wet young woman in a ragged skirt and the other was an equally wet seven-foot-tall blue bloke. Tim was pretty sure he'd seen the blue guy before. *I guess this adventure isn't quite over*, Tim thought.

He nudged Molly. "Don't say I didn't warn you. How much do you want to bet that they want to talk to me?"

Molly's mouth dropped open. "Wh-what is it? Is it a demon? Look at those horns!"

"Nah," Tim said, sounding more sure of himself than he felt. "It's someone from Faerie. The King himself, if I'm not mistaken." *And if his wife, Titania, is any example*, Tim thought, *the royalty of*

*Faerie are a moody and temperamental lot*. Better to just get it over with, he decided.

"Okay," Tim said to them. "What do you want?"

The woman looked startled. "Why would you think we wanted anything?" she asked.

"Well, usually when someone from Faerie shows up, they're looking for me." Tim nodded at the tall blue figure. "We never officially met, King Auberon, but I saw you at your castle once."

King Auberon didn't respond, but the woman beamed. "You are personally acquainted with Lovey-horns? And you have visited his realm? This is wonderful."

"Why?" Tim asked.

"If you've passed between worlds, then you must be acquainted with magic."

"I'll say!" Molly piped up. "Magic is practically his middle name."

"He is a powerful magician," Marya agreed.

"My name is Gwendolyn," the woman said. "Do you think you can help Lovey-horns? You see, his soul is trapped in that globe he is holding, and we'd really like it back where it belongs."

Tim knew he should be surprised; this wasn't the sort of thing a bloke heard every day. *Unless, of course, that bloke is me*, Tim thought.

"How did Auberon's soul wind up in that

crystal ball?" Tim asked. "What is he doing here in the first place? Why isn't he in Faerie?"

"He never told me why he came here," Gwendolyn said. She eyed the unicorn. "I'd guess your magnificent steed also came from that land. Perhaps they came through the same way."

"I don't know how the unicorn got here," Tim said.

"But we're awfully glad he did," Marya said, patting the unicorn. "Did Timothy save your world, too, like mine?" she asked Gwendolyn.

Gwendolyn grinned. "Not that I know of."

"None of this explains how Auberon's soul got stuck in that thing," Tim said.

Gwendolyn bit her lip, and Timothy had the distinct impression that she had something to do with Auberon's predicament.

"Auberon chose to lock up his soul rather than experience his true feelings. But now he is ready to have it back. Please, can't you help?"

Tim knew that there was much more to the situation than Gwendolyn was telling him, but he decided to let it go.

"I—I can try." Tim stepped in front of the imposing regal figure. "King Auberon, I'd like to have your soul, please. I promise I won't break it."

The once proud king's eyes flicked from the globe to Tim, then back to the globe again.

He seemed so lost, his eyes so blank, it made Tim want to fix things for him. *I've become a right regular magical do-gooder*, Tim thought. *I hope trying to solve Auberon's problem doesn't get me into hot water like helping Daniel did.*

"Auberon, you can trust me. I want to help you. I'd like to take a look at that globe."

Gwendolyn cleared her throat. "Er, sir, you'll need to put it into the form of an order or command."

"Auberon, give me the globe," Tim instructed the King.

Slowly, Auberon lifted his head and gazed at Tim with his empty eyes. He handed the globe to Tim.

Tim examined the shiny ball, turning it in his hands. "Let's see. There are little holes in it, like finger sockets in a bowling ball. That must be how the soul goes in. But there's no 'out' that I can see." He glanced up at the rest of the group. "This may sound sort of unmagicianly, but has anyone got a hammer?"

A tiny creature flew by Tim and landed on the globe. Tim recognized him as Amadan, Queen Titania's jester.

"Make that a flyswatter," Tim muttered. Tim remembered Amadan from previous encounters, and he was one nasty critter.

*Uh-oh. If this guy is fluttering around, it's got to be at Titania's bidding.* A worse idea occurred to him. *Or he could be acting as her escort.*

Sure enough, just then Titania, in all her green glory, popped up in front of them. And as usual, she seemed very, very angry.

# Chapter Thirteen

"WHAT STRANGE COMPANY YOU keep these days, my husband," Titania said coldly to Auberon. "One would think you've come far down in the world."

She glared at him as he leaned against the wall, speechless. She crossed her arms and tapped her foot impatiently.

"What?" she demanded, tossing her long hair over her shoulder. "Have you nothing to say to me? I've been looking all over for you."

Still Auberon said nothing. Tim could tell Titania wasn't used to being ignored.

"How dare you treat me this way!" she shouted at her husband.

"Your pardon, miss," Gwendolyn said. "You needn't carry on. Lovey-horns isn't cutting you. It's just that he's missing his soul at the moment."

Titania's eyebrows rose. "Lovey-horns?" she repeated.

Gwendolyn laughed, which definitely angered Titania even more. "That's what I call him. Don't you think it suits him? But don't worry, Timothy will set him right again."

"Timothy?" Titania stared at Gwendolyn. Tim realized that until this moment Titania hadn't even noticed him. So this time she wasn't pursuing him at all—she really had come looking for Auberon. Only now she set her narrowed eyes on Tim.

Every inch of Tim wanted to shrink back into the shadows and sneak away. But he wasn't going to do that with Molly watching. And there was still Auberon's soul to deal with. Marya and Molly had backed up, and the unicorn now stood in front of them, as if it was protecting them. Tim figured the unicorn might have seen Titania in action before.

"What infernal trouble are you up to now?" she demanded. "Haven't you done enough?"

Tim knew she was referring to the death of his true father, Tamlin. Tamlin had sacrificed himself so that Tim could live, and Titania was furious about it.

"I haven't done a thing," Tim protested. "This lady just asked me if I could help, if it's all the same to you."

"He's just trying to do these guys a favor," Molly added. "So back off."

Tim winced. It was nice to have Molly defend him, but not if it got her zapped into another dimension.

But Titania ignored Molly and simply gazed at the globe in Tim's hands. "So is that it?" she asked. She crossed and stood in front of Tim.

"So I hear," Tim replied. He didn't like Titania hovering so close to him. He took a few steps back.

"Auberon's soul is vulnerable in its present state, Timothy," Titania said. "Suggestible."

"Duh," Tim said. Okay, so the attitude was risky, but he was sick of her treating him like an idiot.

"I can protect it as you cannot," she explained. "Give it to me."

"Say 'pretty please.'"

Titania's jaw set, and Tim was fairly sure he saw a vein pop out on her forehead. She was working awfully hard to keep herself under control. Tim wondered what she would do with Auberon's soul once she had it in her possession. Would she really protect it and release it? Or did she just want it as a way to have power over the King of Faerie? Tim wouldn't put anything past her.

Titania's entire manner changed. Tim knew it

had something to do with magic. She made herself as beautiful as she had looked the day he first met her in Faerie. "Bitter words passed between us when we last met, child." Her voice was gentle and soothing.

"Oh, you mean when you threatened my life?" Tim responded. "Yeah, I'd say that conversation was on the bitter side."

"I said much I didn't mean," Titania continued, moving closer. "The grief I felt at Tamlin's passing maddened me for a time." She placed a hand over her heart and bowed her head. "I must ask you to find it in your heart to forgive me."

*Whoa. She must want Auberon's soul really badly to put on such an act.* "Amazing. You do have some manners," Tim commented.

Titania smiled a radiant smile; she practically sparkled. *Yeah, she's definitely doing something magical—a glamour or something.* She held out her hand. "Give me the bauble."

"Sure thing. As soon as you swear on your name that you will really set Auberon's soul free the minute I hand it over." Tim knew that to swear on one's name was the most serious vow anyone magical could make. If Titania were lying, she'd never make such a promise.

Anger and frustration canceled out the glamour Titania was weaving. She instantly reverted to her shrewish, hostile self and lunged at Tim, grabbing for the globe.

"No!" Tim yelped. He stumbled backward, lost his grip on the globe, and it went flying. He flung himself at it, desperate to save it from smashing on the ground. He landed hard on his stomach, his glasses flew off, and his elbows were going to be bruised and scabbed for weeks. But he didn't need his glasses to know that the globe had shattered into a thousand pieces. The smashing sound told him that.

"You accursed changeling!" Titania shrieked. "You destroy everything you touch!"

"*Me?*" Tim said, looking up at her from the pavement. He pushed himself up to a sitting position and placed his glasses back on his nose. "*You* knocked it out of my hands. This is your fault!"

"Silence!" Titania commanded.

Tim's heart pounded, waiting to see what would happen. She had been enraged when Tamlin, her Falconer, had died. How much more furious would she be when it was her own husband in danger?

She stalked toward Tim. "I should have destroyed you myself when I had the chance," she hissed. "Had I known what disasters you would cause me, I would have killed you the minute I gave birth to you."

"Wh-what?" Tim stammered. What was she talking about?

"That's right, changeling," she growled. "First you killed your father. And now, because of what you have done to my husband, Auberon, I, your mother, disown you. You are fatherless *and* motherless."

"You?" Tim's voice came out as a whisper. "You're my mother? How can that be?"

"I may have given birth to you, changeling, but you are no child of mine," Titania said.

Tim sank back on his heels, his mouth open, staring at the Faerie Queen. His mind reeled. Tamlin and Titania were his true parents? This was too big, too huge to contemplate. What about Mary Hunter, lying in the cemetery. The woman Mr. Hunter had married because she had been pregnant—with Tim! Or so he had thought. Tim shook his head, trying to get thoughts to return, but he just felt blank and hollow inside.

A nasty smile spread across Titania's face. "No more smart talk, eh, changeling? And now," she said, her voice growing more powerful, "as you have doomed my lord's soul to limbo, brat, I shall make sure you and your wretched companions join him there!"

Tim saw Titania raise her hands, creating a powerful whirlwind. He knew he should be doing something to stop her—use magic, do anything—but the news that she was his mother had stunned him into a kind of paralysis. He watched her work her magic as if she were very far away, or on telly. Nothing seemed real, least of all himself.

The whirlwind swirled faster and faster, and Tim thought he could see Molly, Marya, and Gwendolyn whirling inside it. It was hard to tell, because they were engulfed in sparkling clouds of magical energy.

Tim moaned, knowing he had failed again.

A voice broke through the clouds. "'Tis a fine display of devotion you make now, my lady."

The whirlwind stopped abruptly, and all was exactly as it had been before. Molly and Marya stood beside the unicorn, Gwendolyn in front of them. Only now Auberon stood towering over Titania.

"You will work no mischief on these good people," he commanded.

"Lovey-horns!" Gwendolyn exclaimed. "Your soul's back where it belongs!"

"My magic has always been stronger than yours, Titania," Auberon said. "It would serve you well to remember that."

"I—I am overjoyed that you were able to return your soul to your body," Titania said. "I was just upset because I feared the clumsy boy had destroyed you."

"You are the only one here who would destroy me," Auberon replied. He gestured to Tim and to Gwendolyn. "These are my teachers."

"Teachers?" Titania scoffed. "What great wisdom can a lord of Faerie hope to learn from such rabble?"

Tim hated to admit it, but Titania had a point.

"What wisdom, my lady asks?" Auberon continued. "To feel without making a fool of myself. To work when it is not enough to wish. To extend oneself in spite of fear or danger. You would do well to learn these lessons yourself."

Titania opened her mouth as if to respond, but unable to think of anything to say, she shut it again.

Auberon turned to Tim. "Did I hear my lady claim you as her own child?"

Tim nodded. "That's what she said."

Auberon glanced back at Titania. "You stand by this, lady? For he is no child of mine."

"He—he is Tamlin's son," Titania replied.

"Ah, yes. Your Falconer."

Tim noticed Auberon didn't seemed surprised or even bothered by that bit of news. *Guess they do things differently in Faerie.*

Auberon lifted Tim's chin. "Aye. I can see Tamlin's mark upon you." He studied Tim's face and looked perplexed. "You say this is your boy?" he asked Titania again, his eyes never leaving Tim's face.

"I have answered you once, husband. Let us not dwell on this."

"Hmmmm," Auberon said. The strangest expression crossed his blue face. Tim could swear the King of Faerie was amused. He released Tim and turned once more to Titania. "We should return now to Faerie," he said. "Thank you all."

Tim watched as the royal couple dematerialized in front of them.

"Wow," Molly murmured. "Just like special effects in the movies."

"Yeah." Tim felt his knees grow weak, and he leaned hard against the alleyway wall. *Too much happens in too short a time*, he decided. Couldn't they spread out these whammies more evenly instead of slamming him all at once?

"Didn't I tell you that Tim was a great magician?" Marya said.

"Are you okay?" Molly asked Tim, touching his arm.

Tim nodded. "I guess. . . ."

"Can you give us a couple of minutes?" Molly asked Marya.

Marya nodded. "Sure. We'll meet you at the ice cream shop."

Tim watched Marya and the unicorn round the corner. He was glad that Molly had asked her to leave them alone. He had a lot to process.

"Listen," Molly said. "What she said about being your mom? I bet it's just one big fat Faerie lie. I wouldn't put anything past that mean green Queen."

"I—I don't know," Tim replied. He looked at her and saw the concern in her brown eyes. It made him feel like he could tell her anything.

"There's something I haven't had a chance to tell you," he confessed. "You know how I found out that my dad wasn't really my dad?"

Molly nodded.

"Well, that was because I discovered who my real father is. Was," he corrected himself. "He's dead now, but when he was alive, his name was Tamlin and he lived in Faerie. In fact, he had the magic to turn himself into a falcon."

Molly let out a low whistle. "Brilliant. I mean, freaky, too, but really brilliant. Can you do that?"

Tim shrugged. "I don't know. I never tried." He shook his head. "So don't you think it makes sense that Titania could actually be my mother?" he asked. "It seems a lot more likely that Tamlin would have a baby with Titania." He gave a bitter laugh. "Ever since I found out, I've been trying to picture my mom with a guy like that. It's been impossible. I mean, how would they have ever even met?"

"I guess that's all true," she agreed. "I don't know, though. Weird stuff happens all the time." She gave him a grin. "You're proof of that!"

Tim couldn't help laughing. Molly always managed to make him feel better. He tried to see the plus side of this latest shocker. "Once Titania calms down, maybe I'll go to Faerie and talk to her. It would be nice to find some sort of family that could help me understand my magic better."

"You don't need her!" Molly assured him. "As far as I can tell, you're doing just fine on your own!"

Tim smiled at her, and as he thought about it, his grin grew even bigger. *Molly's right*, he realized. *I'm doing better each time I try something magical. There may be hope for me yet!*

"You know, all that globe smashing and magic doing really works up an appetite," Tim said. He took Molly's hand firmly in his. "I say, it's time for ice cream. And," he added as they strolled down the street, "since I'm not going to keep any more secrets from you, I have something else to tell you."

"What's that?" Molly asked, concern crossing her face.

Tim grinned. "Well, the whole truth is, I'm flat broke. So you're buying!"

**The journey continues
in *The Books of Magic 5*:
LOST PLACES**

*London, 2022*

THIRTY-TWO-YEAR-OLD Timothy Hunter, the most powerful magical adept of the ages, strolled toward the heavily guarded, massive stone building he called The Formatory. Of course, there were no *visible* guards, but the place was well defended all the same. The protections had been placed by Timothy himself; he'd carved the special runes, chanted the spells in languages long lost, and hung the talismans of great power.

*The demon world provides such handy resources when one has something valuable to protect,* Timothy mused as he climbed the low marble steps. *They should open their own reference library. I'd even donate some of my millions toward its upkeep. Of course,* he thought with a smile, *all I need to do is cast a spell or make a minor threat and any information I want is mine. Or I can always ask Barbatos—he's usually up on the latest incantations and power spells.*

Timothy passed his hand over the gargoyle

guardian on the door and felt the prickly shimmer as the gargoyle's expression changed. One minute it bore a menacing, teeth-bared grimace; the next, a friendly, though still grotesque, smile. The door swung open and Timothy stepped inside the cool, silent building.

"Where does the time go?" Timothy muttered, his footsteps echoing loudly as he crossed the shiny marble floor. "It's been weeks since I paid a visit to the Formatory. Shameful to neglect one's dependents that way, really. And I can't even claim I've been too busy to check on them. The war has been shaping up quite nicely on all fronts, with no more than a nudge here or a tickle there from me." He reached the end of the long hallway and placed his hand on the wall padlock. The steel door clanged open.

He hesitated on the threshold. "Be a man, Hunter," he admonished himself. "You thought you were done here, didn't you? You could have sworn you'd finally got her right."

Timothy straightened his tie, pushed his glasses back up the bridge of his nose, and raked his fingers through his short dark hair. He cupped his hand to check his breath, then stepped into the room. The Molly room.

He stood under the sparkling chandelier in the large circular room and slowly turned, gazing at each of the Mollys. They gazed back from behind their glass walls, separated from one another by thick, soundproof marble barriers. There was Molly as a teenager in jeans, heavy work boots, and black T-shirt. There was a slightly older Molly in an evening gown, a Molly dressed like a biker chick, a Molly in the latest fashion. Molly after Molly after Molly—and not one of them was quite right.

Each Molly moved up to her glass barrier, imploring him silently for . . . what? Attention? Approval? Freedom?

Timothy remained unresponsive to all those pairs of identical brown eyes.

"You thought you were all set to ride off into the sunset with the new-and-improved Molly, didn't you?" Timothy muttered darkly. "Like in some sentimental movie, complete with violins scraping in the background and not a dry eye in the house as the picture fades." He shook his head in disgust. "Jerk."

He slowly paced the circle of Mollys. "You're too romantic for your own good," he scolded himself. "Surely you ought to know by now that these things take time." He stopped in front of a Molly in a soft, flowered dress with ruffles on the hem. "Speaking of which, how long has this little peach been ripening?"

This Molly's eyes were filled with tears. *She must be awed by my presence*, Timothy surmised. *Unless* . . . He peered at her more closely, and she lowered her eyes. *Unless she was crying before I came into the room. That will never do.* Expressing unhappiness at her situation could not be tolerated. It signified discontent—disapproval.

He pressed the buttons on the pad beside the door. It beeped when he'd completed the sequence, and the glass panel in front of the weeping Molly slid open. The Molly looked startled and took a step back as Timothy moved into her confined area.

"Hello, Molly," he said gently. She seemed a bit skittish and he didn't want to frighten her. "I'm sorry, but you'll have to remind me. How long have you been here?"

The Molly kept her eyes down, and Timothy could see her tremble. A harsh voice behind her answered his question.

"Three years, four months, seven days, and fifteen minutes to be precise."

Timothy's gaze left the Molly and flicked to the wizened old creature coming to stand behind her. Vuall. She was teacher, governess, and prison guard rolled into one withered husk of a woman. Even taller than Timothy, she had a skull-like face covered in wrinkles, and her steel-gray hair was pulled into a tight bun on top of her head. The only jewelry she wore was long, dangling chains as earrings, and Timothy had never seen her in anything other than the old-fashioned black dress she always wore. Not quite human, not quite demon, Vuall had been around as long as there were girls needing to be kept in check. Girls to be properly trained. She was someone who could enforce all those unspoken rules that made girls fit into the molds created for them, no matter how much the girls resisted.

"Miss O'Reilly. Didn't you hear Timothy ask you a question?" Vuall demanded in a voice that sounded like chalk grating on a blackboard. "Come now, you minx," she admonished the Molly. "Can you tell Master Timothy Hunter in all honesty that you feel yourself worthy to be the object of his devotion?"

"No, miss," the Molly answered in a whisper.

Vuall sniffed disdainfully. "Quite right. Which means we must continue with our lessons. And what are they today?"

The Molly looked slightly perplexed and then responded, "Needlepoint, miss? And piano and French?"

Vuall's eyes narrowed to the size of raisins. "And . . . ?"

"And holding very still, miss? And smiling."

"Very good." Vuall turned to Timothy. "As you can see, she isn't ready yet."

"Yes, yes." Timothy waved a hand. "I'll leave you to your work."

He stepped back out of the chamber. He ignored the pleading eyes of the other Mollys as he left the Molly room and strode out of the Formatory.

*She may not be quite there yet*, Timothy mused, *but she does seem to be coming along prettily. Vuall should be finished with her soon enough. After that little outburst from the new Molly last night, well, a replacement was certainly called for.*

Yes, the Molly in the flowered dress might do very well. She was a bit younger than the one at home, Timothy observed, closer to the age Molly had been when she . . . well, when *he* had discovered that perhaps she didn't completely share his feelings or his vision and he realized he needed to make improvements.

He shook his head as he walked up the path toward his mansion. *It shouldn't be this difficult.* He felt annoyance rise at the unfairness of it all. *Why is it that the wars I wage seem so much simpler than training a Molly to behave as I wish?*

Timothy flicked his hand at the door, expecting it to open as it always did. Only this time . . . it didn't. He stopped and stared. He tried again.

Then again. With a grunt and a great deal of effort, he tried once more, and finally the door responded, flinging itself open. Timothy jogged up the steps, filled with some nameless energy, and stomped into the mansion.

"Have to look into that," he muttered, staring back at the door as it slammed shut behind him. *Why do I have the nagging feeling that the world is running a bit offtrack today?*

"Good morning, sweetheart," a Molly said. She sat precisely where he had left her—perched on the sofa, wearing her pink silk dress and sparkling jewels. "Is—is something the matter?"

*I hate that hesitating speech pattern she's developed,* Tim thought with fury. "Haven't I told you not to yammer at me while I'm thinking? You can see that I'm thinking, can't you?"

"Oh, yes." The Molly's face flushed. "I'm sorry, sweetheart."

"I'll give you sorry, you stupid cow—if you don't shut your mouth." Timothy strode past her, needing to get away from her.

*She is far too docile,* Timothy decided. *Except when she isn't! Oh, why can't she be what I want her to be?*